Lamplighter

Lamplighter

Kerry Donovan Brown

Victoria University Press

TE WHARE WĀNANGA O TE ŪPOKO O TE IKA A MĀUI

VICTORIA
UNIVERSITY OF WELLINGTON

VICTORIA UNIVERSITY PRESS
Victoria University of Wellington
PO Box 600 Wellington
vup.victoria.ac.nz

National Library of New Zealand Cataloguing-in-Publication Data

Donovan Brown, Kerry.
Lamplighter / Kerry Donovan Brown.
ISBN 978-0-86473-916-2
I. Title.
NZ821.3—dc 23

Published with the support of a grant from

creative
nz
ARTS COUNCIL OF NEW ZEALAND *TOI AOTEAROA*

Printed in China by 1010 Printing International

For Celine, Paul,
Sam, and Dylan

Old World lamplighters once lit the streets of cities like Constantinople, Alexandria and Rome. In the countryside, in the new colonies, the Lamplighter doesn't light passages through the dark; he lights perimeters against it, and the wildernesses beyond.

—Emerald Tapuwai, concerning the diminishment of Ignis Xavier Gullstrand

(seeing the GHOST) Avaunt, and quit my sight! Let the earth hide thee.
Thy bones are marrowless, thy blood is cold.
Thou hast no speculation in those eyes
Which thou dost glare with!

—*Macbeth*

The River Bridge

AT THE TRIVIUM, where the mainroad, the river bridge and the stopbank meet, the Lamplighter lights his last lamp of the evening. That last cage of fire casts up on the cool concrete underbelly of the bridge, illuminating graffiti,—

Go Homo!

The Lamplighter's grandson, who has a head torch and the residue of a nosebleed, pretends it is intended as an endorsement, and not an instruction, or threat.

From under the bridge the Lamplighter whistles. He has spotted a stray out ankle-deep in the river, nosing at a heap of dumped rubbish. He calls to it, but it won't come to him. It raises its hackles and trots off into the scrub. Now the Lamplighter is in a bad mood. He loves dogs.

'C'mon, Candle,' he growls.

Candle isn't his grandson's real name, just what he's called for tonight and nights like tonight. It's short for Candlewick, the name for an apprentice lamplighter. Lamplighters are called other names, like Laternarius, and the Nightwatchman, and Will-o'-the-wisp. Lucifer maybe, which means 'light bearer'.

Candle feels in his coat. He has armed himself with a number of talismans. He has a citrine amethyst set in a silver ring. A tail feather from a swamp harrier. In his pockets are hard green tomatoes his mum has picked for him to eat. The most potent talisman is a great white shark tooth.

The Lamplighter is walking back through the lamplight, but Candle would like to stay a moment longer. Trivium means 'place where three roads meet'. It's not a real trivium; the mainroad doesn't stop at the bridge, it continues on the other side of the river. And the stopbank begins again, beyond the bridge, to protect other inland settlements against rising waters. Candle has allowed himself this interpretation though, allowed himself to believe that three ways through the world meet here.

He moves his torch to the crevices and the undergrowth of the bridge. Across a carpet of periwinkle and old man's beard, an empty soft drink bottle, a tiny pair of blue underpants. More writing on a concrete support says,—

Bob. Sidney. Rohan. Jeice.

They must be like him. Pilgrims to this most beautiful place. Candle noses at a sooty fire pit with his shoe—here's where they make their sacrifices. Next time he'll bring something to write his name with. Next time he'll bring a sacrifice.

He listens to a stock truck rush by overhead. He pictures the carriages filling with the breath and bodies of sheep. In his pocket the tooth feels like a piece of cold crystal smoke. Candle traces its serrated edge with his fingertip.

The Stopbank

'Do you know how many people have been killed out in the wetlands over the years, Granddad?'

'Nah,' the Lamplighter spits back.

Candle can tell he doesn't like that he asked. Doesn't like how Candle is working his way up to something. Treading on his turf. The Lamplighter's part in life is to be chief storyteller. His apprentice's part in life is to learn these stories, and to figure them out—so he can tell the stories properly, when it's his turn.

'Hundreds, I reckon,' says Candle.

The Lamplighter shrugs and sticks out his lower lip. If his favourite stories are anything to go by, the wetland has claimed many lives. In his stories the river is dangerous.

Gravel crunches underfoot. They're walking back through the Lamplighter's lamplight. Back towards the village and the sea. Candle can hear the river through the willow forest. It's the end of the wet season and it's full. Its ill-defined edges have joined with the marshes. Saltwater Creek has grown heavy and caramel-coloured. The current moves like a leech riding across the surface of mud.

'Do you know about that escaped wolf?' says Candle.

'There are no wolves in this country.' His voice is thin and prickly.

'Officially there aren't. But the circus smuggled one in. Rib told me,' Candle adds.

The Lamplighter picks at a bloody spot between his jaw and ear.

'Ribby's a crafty bugger,' he says.

Rib was once apprentice to the Lamplighter. Treading the perimeters between worlds can be a risky business, with one foot in the wilderness, one foot in civilisation. Apprentices are supplied to lamplighters, to carry their apparatus, to bear witness to their exploits, to share their burden. To remember their stories.

'Rib said they called it Wolf of the Ethiopian Wastes, and Doggod,' says Candle. 'He said it wasn't really a dog or a wolf. When they caught her she had tattooed ears.'

The Lamplighter grins,—

'That means she was the pet of some voodoo bitch.'

'Yeah.' Candle smiles back. 'Rib said that too.'

Candle remembers Rib telling him. His bare limbs warming up in the sunlight—the cobweb-like scar tissue on his ruined arm glistening.

'Rib said that the doggod copies human speech,' Candle tells his grandfather. 'It's a perfect mimic. It called out to Rib from its cage: *Look, mum! Come see! Come!*'

The old man is looking away, but Candle can tell he is listening.

'*No closer, sweetheart*, the doggod would call. *No. Closer, sweetheart. Closer.*

'Rib said the doggod would call out to him in his own voice,' says Candle. '*Come to me!* Then it would bark and its voice was like the crack of a whip.'

The Lamplighter has gone quiet. It's very dark. Candle kicks at the gravel as they walk, to scare away hedgehogs. Ahead some of the lamps have gone out, creating a pool of darkness over the floodgate. Candle bumps shoulders with his granddad.

'It listens to people talking,' says Candle. 'It remembers the names it hears to use later, to lure its prey out of safety, calling them into caves, or secluded places. It used its voices on Rib the night it got out.'

The Lamplighter is silent. Candle holds onto his shark tooth for power.

'Come to me, Ignis!' Candle calls out, using his grandfather's Christian name.

'Hah,' he says. 'Fuck off, Candle.'

The Lamplighter lurches forward blindly, toward the floodgate and its seething trap of swamp water. Candle falls back. The light at the end of the Lamplighter's pole whirls above him, like a satellite in a bad orbit, or a moth on fire.

Bog Crescent

A school of angelfish, black with silver marbling and orange eyes, navigates the limits of the living room aquarium. The centre of their world is a piece of petrified bogwood on which a number of water ferns have fastened their roots. Each angelfish is the size of a pocket mirror, with long trailing fins. If one turns sideways it becomes invisible against the Amazonian water grasses. Once there were seven, but one vanished overnight—just its bones left; translucent slivers on the pebbled bottom.

MERV AND WAVERLY DE VOL are the hosts. Classical music is playing softly on the radio. All their seats, the armchairs, and the wooden stools from the dining room, have been pulled back to the fringes of the lounge, as well as the extras that have been brought along in the backseats of cars, mostly piano seats, footrests, a beanbag or two. In the cleared space there's only a crate with a cushion. On top of that sits Emerald Tapuwai with no clothes on, encircled by the villagers.

Her breasts are surprising. Non-symmetrical, partly collapsed, like cakes taken out of the oven too early, with raisiny nubs as well. Female nipples are latches, Candle is reminded, for little mouths. At least that's how they're designed. He's not sure if Emerald has used hers for feeding babies, but they're certainly large enough to be taken hold of. Her hair is long and crimped, and she's gathered it up on top of her head, holding it there, her elbows pointing to the ceiling. The hair on her head is dull burgundy. Candle can't bring his eyes to the triangle of fur between her legs, but her hips are prodigious and freckled. The glow of the bar heater beside her has turned her calves traffic-cone orange.

Merv, standing languidly by the feature fish tank, his eyes half closed, says, 'Okay, now a five-minute pose to finish off.' Emerald drops her arms, switches position on her plinth, and places her hands together in her lap. It's a comfortable arrangement to finish on, not only for Emerald. Her limbs are gathered together, like a flower closing, and her breasts are held plump between her upper arms. Candle works swiftly, although around him bones are cracking, and villagers are already blowing on their easels as if to finish.

After five minutes, Merv and Waverly bring out trays of olives and pickles and pineapple skewered on toothpicks and Waverly memorises orders for tea and coffee.

Emerald slips into a teal green dressing gown with a dragon embroidered on it. She begins to mingle, taking in all the new likenesses of herself, smiling, but not speaking.

Candle has drawn her breasts, suspended in negative space, over and over. He's not too embarrassed when Emerald leans in to see.

'Mammary studies,' he offers. Emerald looks closely, and smiles until her eyes and mouth are three creased slits. There are glossy half circles under her eyes, like the insides of certain seashells.

'Emerald,' cries Barbara Grig, the village shopkeeper. 'Take a look at this. You don't look your best!' Barb shakes out a huge sheet of paper, which she has filled to the corners with charcoal markings. Her thinly applied lipstick is smudged with black dust. 'I've spaced your eyes too far apart,' she says. When Emerald moves to investigate, Barb whistles to Candle, 'Can you come in to work Friday, five to eight? Yes?'

The lounge is teeming with shopkeepers of the past and present. Barb's predecessor, Seabright Durivage, is here. She shifts her heavy-seeming eyeglasses and says to Candle, 'Good to see you.' Her husband Romuald squeezes Candle's hip as he inches through to the kitchen—an old habit of his, squeezing, inching, pinching. Candle can see another former shopkeeper, Judi or Julie, who ran the shop when Candle was still a child. She's talking to Pan Ahn, the crabber. Her eyeglasses have blue-tinted lenses, in front of a perm like a nimbus. Valerie Weatherly sits by the piano with her austere and wrinkled husband beside her. She's wearing pearls and a grey suede eye patch. Valerie sips from a glass mug with a lemon slice poaching inside. Kemp Tibald, who spends his entire pension at the shop, on marked-up cans of beetroot, asparagus, condensed milk, and bottle after bottle of crabapple wine, is rapping his cane on the wooden floor, louder and louder, until finally calling out, 'Let's have it then, shall we?'

Candle watches Sigi Ahn, the crabber's grandnephew, put down his pencil and get up—his Alsatian is scratching at the sliding doors that open out on the deck. Sigi tugs at Candle's shoulder as he passes by and says, 'Smoke?'

Candle follows him to the curtained sliding doors and they slip out together. Sigi slides the doors shut behind them. The back lawn is in darkness, the slate stepping stones that lead through the grass to the washing line catch what little light there is. There's a glasshouse, a back fence, beyond that the stopbank, the creek, the wetlands. The Alsatian scrambles to Sigi, its breath hot and huge, its tail doing big circles.

'Settle down, girl,' Sigi says, and she does, resting her head in his lap. Sigi has a big lap, and a big head set with solemn, lovely eyes. He and Candle went to primary school together, and some of high school before Sigi was expelled for fighting. He has big arms, and on one bicep a new tattoo, which he shows Candle after lighting his cigarette.

'It's a flame in the shape of a heart,' he says. 'In honour of your granddad.'

Somebody opens the sliding door a crack, but doesn't come out. It's getting stuffy inside.

'If our hosts would take verses one and two,' Emerald is saying, 'and Kemp, perhaps you'd like to follow them with verse three?'

'Aye aye, ma'am,' comes Kemp's reply, nearer to the door.

Candle is looking at the flaming heart. A long moment passes. Sigi grins and flexes his bicep. The tattoo tightens over the bulge of muscle.

'We give thanks,' calls Merv, beginning the village ode. 'We give thanks to the Lamplighter, who plugged a split seam in the stopbank where the flood had breached.'

'The night, the flood, is black, is foul,' calls back Emerald.

Sigi is still flexing, but now he drops his arm and glances at the gap in the doors, listening.

'We give thanks,' calls Waverly, 'to the Lamplighter, who slew the shark that stole the child who swam at the crook of Saltwater Creek.'

'The night, the flood, is black, is foul.' Other voices join Emerald's.

The cuff of Sigi's T-shirt slips back over his bicep, obscuring the heart. Candle reaches out to move it back aside.

Kemp Tibald calls out, 'Thanks, to the Lamplighter, who extinguished the swamp fires, and so spared the pasture,—

'The night, the flood, is black, is foul.'

Candle holds his hand against the flaming heart on Sigi's arm. He races ahead of the chanters, he has all the verses memorised,—

Thanks to the Lamplighter, who shovelled the sludge, who guarded the gate, who felled the trees, who poured the wine, who shot the goat, who burned the oil, who drained the cup, who pickled the fruit, who speared the snake, who walked the dark road—

'Who held the swamp at bay,' says Candle. He squeezes Sigi's bicep.

'The night, the flood, is black, is foul.'

Sigi gently swipes at Candle's hand, as if flicking a caterpillar from his skin.

'Avaunt, Wet Pete,' cry the villagers, all together.

'Porbeagle will go to the dogs without your granddad,' says Sigi, getting up. 'That's what my uncle says.'

He's turning away from the glow of the curtains. Candle can't see his face. Sigi Ahn steps into the dark of the side of the house, and walks away, the toenails of his dog clattering on the cobbles.

Inside, after the village meeting, Candle helps Waverly De Vol with the supper dishes. She washes, he dries. Her shoulder-length hair has greyed, with only strands of what must be her original hair colour. Dull black, or peat brown. Candle watches her through the corners of his eyes as she dips teacups and empty pickle jars into the suds. Waverly seems as wrung out as the Lamplighter tells Candle she is. He says she was once happier, before Wet Pete took away her happiness.

When he's gathering his things to leave, Emerald Tapuwai, with a coat over her dressing gown and gumboots on her feet, puts her hand on his shoulder, and says his name.

'Candle,' she says, 'take this.'

She hands him an unsealed envelope with the edge of a newspaper clipping showing. On the envelope is written *For Sylla*.

Saltwater Creek

Sylla sometimes uses an antenna.

Something is wrong with her eyes. Now and again the pupils dilate until they nearly eclipse the iris, leaving only a thin pale green perimeter. Too much light can get in, she says, and she can't see well. When her condition is at its worst, her pupillary sphincters—those glassy green muscles—collapse, a capillary ruptures, and she weeps like a stuck tap.

On the creek bank,—

Her feet dangle. She drinks the salt from the mud with her toes.

'You know,' says Sylla, on a blanket, picking grass, 'you're the last of your kind now. You are functionally extinct.'

Candle is watching the bulrushes move on the other side of the creek, waiting for a bittern to move, or his favourite kind of crab. He turns his head to his mother. She's wearing a pair of pinhole sunglasses, a faded brown dress, that's all. Her antenna is detached, lifeless beside her.

'That's an interesting way to put it, Mum,' he replies.

Candle is eighteen, the same age as Sylla was when she gave birth to him. That makes her thirty-six. Some of the villagers say they could be siblings. At eighteen, Candle is a young apprentice to an old lamplighter. His grandfather hadn't produced the son he had hoped for. Instead Sylla arrived, and then her sisters. The Lamplighter had waited for a grandson, and when Sylla succeeded in delivering him one, he had waited for Candle to come of age. When Candle was eleven, and still too young, the Porbeagle village council insisted the Lamplighter take another apprentice, in case he should expire on the dark road, and take with him his years of experience. Rib was given to the Lamplighter, supplied by his aunty Emerald Tapuwai, the villagehead. When Rib quit his apprenticeship, and could not be persuaded to return to the post, the council reluctantly agreed to allow the Lamplighter's grandchild to begin training. By then, even in the frontier places, where old traditions are precious and robust, lamplighters were disappearing.

'Don't tell me you're not relieved, love,' says Sylla to Candle. 'I'm relieved for you, now that it's official.' Sylla returns the clipping to the envelope, and folds the envelope in half.

'I'm relieved,' says Candle.

Sylla can feel the weight of her husband's binoculars in Candle's hands. After a moment she says to him,—

'Your Granna taught me fear, like all mothers should teach their young.'

This is how she always begins her sessions with Candle. Women, to whom fearing comes naturally, are tasked with tutoring apprentices on the subject.

'Fear of electric sockets,' expands Sylla. 'Fear of strangers, fear of poisonous things under the sink. Your grandmother reaffirmed fears in me that are probably instinctual, like fire, spiders, the dark—and special fears, particular to Porbeagle.

'For example, when I was a girl I'd walk along the swampbrink and feel the choppy edges of everything,' says Sylla. 'There's the marshland, rogue currents, king tides. I'd walk along the stopbank and see the giant bodies of crashed-down willows, and a current disappearing swiftly under a clogged bank, and white swarms of mosquito larvae in a stagnant pool, and water plants grown all across a channel, so that you might step into it and disappear in a wink. I'd see a distant person on the riverbed looking my way. These are some of Porbeagle's fearful things.'

Overhead a kanuka branch creaks.

'When it came to things to be afraid of, your grandmother touched on a variety. It's still her favourite subject.' Sylla rolls onto her back.

Candle sees through the binoculars, pressing his eyes into the soft rubber eye rests. The marsh grasses wobble as he shifts the focus. He sees something.

'What is it?'

Sylla feels her son startle beside her. She takes off her protective glasses, and tries to see. Her eyeballs swell. The creek, a maze of bulrushes, the stopbank, all light up, and then fade to white. A grey kanuka branch lingers in her periphery, close enough to reach, before dissipating.

'It's okay, Mum. Somebody's in the grasses. A crabber probably.'

'Where's my feeler?' Her pupils are blown. Inside her an optic mechanism, or maybe part of her brain, has liquefied. Her pupils have grown enormous. She presses a finger to the corner of each eye, as if to clear away sleep. She wipes and her fingertips come away a little red.

Her antenna is on the blanket beside her. It's a long white willow stem, sea polished, and bumpy in places. Candle picked it off the beach with her in mind. There's a ball-shaped fishing float attached to the tip. Sylla uses it like a rigid tentacle, to check her surroundings, testing the surfaces where she is walking.

Up on the stopbank, behind Sylla and Candle's spot under the kanuka trees, a man wearing a high-vis vest has stopped. He's crouching with a measuring tape. Candle watches as he rattles a can of spray paint and then, with a fizz and a puff, leaves a mark on the ground.

'Oh, there it is,' says Sylla, finding her antennae and lifting it up in the air. 'A feeler can be a weapon too. It can have a sting.'

Porbeagle Row

CANDLE'S DAD built the house himself, when Candle was just a baby. Sylla has photographs of Gil taken then. A head of curls and a lopsided smile, poised at the top of a ladder, and straggling bare roof beams, feigning hammer swings for the camera below him.

Tonight the windows are all open. Every window is hung with layers of net curtains to diffuse sunlight, and they billow from all the openings and from the gap left in the sliding doors. Leaf litter from the grapevines that grow along the eaves blows inside, along with chicken feathers that tickle Sylla's bare ankles as she turns about the kitchen. Clumps of sea lilies—part plant, part animal— sit in a colander under a running tap. A big pot of white sauce simmers on the stove. With a blunt kitchen knife Sylla bashes apart ginger root, parsley and dill, and several small onions. She's making her own recipe, *pot-du-lys*. She tells her husband this means 'lily stew' in French. She always cooks late. Sylla is most active in the mornings and evenings.

In the kitchen there's a large piece of particleboard attached to the wall. There's a calendar pinned to it now, and various notes written in red felt-tip. There are recipes of course, and a rectangle of yellow card, which Sylla has decorated using her coloured pencils and a calligraphy pen. On it is written: *The night, the flood, is black, is foul.*

When Candle was much younger, Sylla would help him up onto the bench and they'd use the drawing pins to copy real-life constellations onto the particleboard. Sylla could remember many of them by heart. Cetus the Whale, and Berenice's Hair, and Canis Major. Scorpius, with a red pin at its heart. The red pin represents the red star, Antares. Sometimes they'd invent their own constellations; the red pin would become the good eye of Valerie Weatherly, or the bullet wound through the middle of one of Gil's shelducks, or, sometimes, the light at the end of the Lamplighter's pole.

Tonight Antares is by itself. A space has been cleared for a small clipping from the local newspaper, shrivelled as if it once was saturated, and the red star stabbed through its middle,—

PORBEAGLE LAMPLIGHTER TO RETIRE AT CHRISTMAS:— Emerald Tapuwai, Porbeagle villagehead, has announced the retirement of long-serving Lamplighter Ignis X. Gullstrand, who acceded to the post in 1943 (preceded by Lamplighter Otneil Stambler) and has lit lamps along the swampbrink for close to a half-century thereafter. Ms. Tapuwai has revealed that the mantle will be dissolved, thus ending the historic employ of a lamplighter in the village. Friends and nostalgists are invited for a festivity in honour and conclusion of Gullstrand's service to the community, on December 24, Porbeagle Hall, from eventide until late.

After Candle eats he undresses for a bath.

Gil says from the other side of the bathroom door, 'Don't be all night in there, boy.'

The bath is yellow, with claws mounted on balls, which have pressed holes in the lino. While it fills Candle tries to get an impression of his whole body in the small cabinet mirror above the sink. The only full-length mirror in the house is in his parents' bedroom, and it isn't often he can steal glances of himself in there. He looks for new kinks in his body, whorls of fine hairs, for fresh evidence of his manhood. The mirror fogs over after a moment, and he gives up. He shuts off the tap, and bit by bit lowers himself into the hot water.

The water has cooled and he's about to hop out when the Lamplighter turns up at the back door. The bathroom window is open a crack, and Candle can hear him moving around before he knocks. Quick, naked and dripping wet, Candle switches off the bathroom light and stands still. Granddad must've stopped by on his way back from the river bridge. He's had a few drinks as well, Candle can tell. This isn't the first time he's called by late in the evening. On the nights he goes solo on the swampbrink he can get a bit lonely. Starved for attention, Sylla would say. Tonight it might be different. Tonight it might be about his retirement.

The Lamplighter bangs on the back door, a moment later he bangs again, but Sylla isn't answering. Candle can hear her pacing the kitchen instead, stomping and swearing to herself, at Candle's dad.

'Sylla, answer your door!' calls the Lamplighter. 'They've

had enough of me, the ungrateful bastards!' When she doesn't answer,—'Sylla, you bitch!'

Candle stands still in the dark. He finds a towel.

'You're a fucking bitch, Sylla!'

'Fuck off, prick,' says Sylla from the kitchen, loud enough for Candle to hear.

Granddad bangs again. Sylla storms towards the door. Candle imagines her breaking away from the arms of Gil. 'Fuck—*off*,' she screams at the back door.

Candle hears Sylla's bedroom door slam shut. Gil sighs and a moment later turns on the outside light and opens the back door. From the bathroom window Candle watches his dad give the Lamplighter a hand up from where he's planted himself in the rosemary bush.

'Ignis,' Gil mutters. 'Ignis, Ignis, Ignis.'

The Lamplighter staggers to his son-in-law, his left shoulder bouncing off Gil's right—it's something like an embrace.

Gil says, 'Come on, mate,' and leads him off the property, back to his house-on-stilts.

Afterwards Sylla dries Candle's hair, with her hairdryer, in her bedroom.

This is Sylla's bedroom,—

The vanity dresser was a wedding gift from the village. A box of tissues set inside a handmade cushioned box. Her jewellery is silver and diamond-cut citrine quartz her sister brought back from India. Pottles of night cream, and day cream. Tweezers. An empty bottle of perfume with a crocheted hand pump and tassels. A hand mirror.

The River Mouth

WHEN GIL ASKS IF CANDLE would like to go out with him, fishing, or for a hunt, or to the shops, he asks while he's not facing Candle, as if in passing, with something like shyness. Like he's had to work himself up to ask.

'Candle,' he says, 'Keeley and me are going out to drag the net. Do you want to come?'

Does he want me to come, wonders Candle. It's hard to tell.

'Yep, Dad,' he says, 'I will.'

'Get ready, then. Put on boots. Put on a jacket. Eat some breakfast.' Candle's dad is more confident giving instructions than he is with invitations.

Candle climbs into the back of Keeley Samuelson's four-wheel drive, with the dragnet, which is in a heap pinned down by Keeley's black lab, Jess. There's a sack for the fish, and a vat of slushy ice to bury the sack in once it's full. Gil and Keeley get in the front. Both of their faces are lined like tuatua shells, and under their caps they're both beginning to lose their hair.

The jeep leaves the village through the willow forest fiord, driving down onto the riverbed, choosing one of the bumpy clay tracks through the scrubland. The two men don't bother to notice the rabbits, but Jess and Candle prick up their ears and follow their progress ahead of them, until they scramble off the road, leaping into the gorse. Gil mutters, 'Get out of the road, rabbit.'

The track takes them out of the scrub and the horizon opens onto the flats, an expanse of compacted pebbles, cockleshells and fossil-silt. They're between two arms of the braided river; the mouth is still ahead of them. To their right, on the other side of the lagoon, stands the house on stilts—a five-minute walk across the water surface, though it has taken fifteen minutes to drive around to this side.

'There's Ignis,' says Gil. 'He said he'd meet us out here.'

Away across the flats they can see a lone figure. A mirage moves beneath him, maybe a hundred tiny crabs, sidestepping into their burrows.

'Dad, what about last night? What about what he said to Mum?'

'Just cool it, son.'

This whole thing could be an exercise in consoling the Lamplighter, realises Candle. The truck hits a bump and Candle's head bumps the roof.

'Bloody grave markers,' says Keeley.

'Better stop then,' says Gil. 'Better respect the dead.'

This far out on the mudflat there is a burial ground.

'More or less a hundred years ago there was a battle at the swampbrink, some say a massacre,' goes the Lamplighter's story. 'The tribespeople who once lived where Porbeagle is now were attacked by marauders, led by the warrior chieftain, Te Rauparaha. The defending tribe took a stand here on the flats, but they were overwhelmed. Some were able to retreat into the wetland, but many of them were killed. Afterwards, missionary settlers laid a river boulder overtop every fallen body they discovered here on the flats.'

Across the fossil-silt stand many stones. At least a

hundred. Candle knows this story by heart. He has learnt nearly all the Lamplighter's stories.

The truck stops and they all get out. Gil and Keeley put on rubber waders that go right up their bodies, and are held on by straps, like overalls. They take some time untangling and laying out the twenty-five-metre dragnet. It's braided nylon, with lead weights along the bottom, and corks on top to keep it afloat. They clean the net, picking out dried up seaweed.

Candle takes a walk amongst the headstones, all of them lumpy and mud-slathered. The crown of one is speckled with barnacles; another is almost entirely covered in pink lichen. No two are alike. He passes Bianca, Jacques, Sigi and Florent. The missionaries renamed the bodies underneath—as a sort of christening maybe, or binding spell—and then swiftly began building cottages on the old pā site, cauterising the wounds in the earth with cottages and onion patches. It became tradition amongst the old Porbeagle families to name their newborns after one of the missionary stones. Sylla is out here. So is Ignis.

'Some of them are missing,' Candle says. 'I can't see Walvis, or Voilet, or Leander.'

'Salt air is corrosive to these old headstones,' says Gil, as if in answer.

'Liquefaction could've sunk 'em,' offers Keeley.

The missionary stones thin out. Jess whirls about the flat, running in big figure-eights. Candle watches out for algae slicks, and sinkholes, and the stranded, stretched-out bodies of bluebottles. He reaches the river, slightly behind the other two. Today the water is the same shade of grey as the sand. The clouds bruise against one another on the horizon. The Lamplighter approaches.

'G'day, Ignis,' says Gil.

Keeley touches the brim of his cap and says a word through his moustache.

The Lamplighter spits on the sand.

Gil and Keeley are both well built, if a little lean, a little pliant. Granddad is made of thicker stuff. He receives their greetings in silence, like a totem. The two younger men begin to spread out the net on the riverbank. The Lamplighter and Candle watch.

'Yep,' says the Lamplighter, and points them to where the river broadens into the sea. 'It's bloody rough.'

Gil steps into the river. He's taking the deep end. If he has communicated a plan of action to Keeley, Candle didn't hear it. They must have a secret language of nods and mutterings. They must read each other's eyes.

The net stretches into the water as Gil leads it out. The water is up to his middle. Keeley moves into the shallows. They pull through the river in the direction of the ocean— they need to be quicker than the current. Candle doesn't know how long they will drag it for, or what tells them to stop dragging.

When they come to shore, they stay a net-length away from each other. They lay it down flat on the sand; things are struggling in dark tangled spots. Candle darts forward.

While Gil and Keeley inspect the flounder—checking their sizes on a pocket tape measure—Candle begins setting free the tangled-up paddle crabs. It's intricate work, as their segmented legs and pincers are easily entangled in the mesh. Gil doesn't have the same patience for them as Candle does, but he doesn't mind spending the few extra minutes to free them. Some of the crabs have markings on the shells of their backs that look like human faces. The Lamplighter likes to say they're copies of the people who died in the massacre.

Candle works on one crab, crouching. He holds on to the edges of its back-plate with one hand, holding it away from the net, and with the other hand he tries to ease the individual cords from its chitinous limbs. He nearly has it free. The crab's eyestalks are flattened to its shell, its legs held out straight—it might understand Candle's good intentions.

'The sack, Candle,' calls Gil. He and Keeley are ready with the fish.

Candle leaves the crab, and retrieves the sack from where he left it under a river stone. Jess is sniffing at the feet of the men, where the green-grey flounder are flapping about on the sand. They have speckled markings on their backs as well—eyespots, maybe—but the Lamplighter doesn't have anything to say about it. He sniffs and steps away. Candle helps collect the fish into the sack. They're very soft and slick to handle; their fins at the fringes of their flat bodies and their gill covers are their only parts that have an edge to them. The goo that coats their bodies comes off on the palms of his hands and gets in between his fingers. Candle would prefer to euthanase them before they go into the sack, but Gil says they stay fresher if allowed to die intact.

Candle turns back to the net. His grandfather is there, standing where Candle was a few moments ago. He reaches down and takes hold of the crab—his foot pressed to the net it's entangled in. He tears the crab from the net, as if he's pulling out a weed. There's a tiny sound, nearly inaudible, as its exoskeleton is torn into several pieces.

'Bait,' says the Lamplighter, and tosses the remains into the ocean.

Gil and Keeley decide to take the net out into the surf.

They stay in the river, working their way to the ocean. Candle follows the Lamplighter across an expanse of low dunes onto the beach. When Gil and Keeley break from the river mouth they bring the net around in an arc, pulling it through the ocean in a sweep that will bring them back to shore. Candle is nervous to see the men work the net through this new body of water. The whitecaps break over their shoulders, filling up their rubber waders from the top, and every so often a swell larger than the rest will roll in and lift the men right up from the seabed. He's relieved when they make for the shore, but Jess is agitated, whining and fussing in their direction. Gil and Keeley are struggling with the net, straining to drag it through into the shallows.

'What is it?' Candle says to himself, or to Jess.

The Lamplighter mutters something. Candle thinks he hears him say, 'I can feel him moving.'

Candle stares into the waves. The men heave the net through a whitecap, and then, at the centre of the net, a huge glistening black hump breaks the surface. Whatever it is surges forward, stops, submerges, and then explodes upwards, sending up sprays of seawater. It can't break through the net.

Gil and Keeley have their backs to the beach and are pulling the net with all their might. They make some ground, and the thing in the net loses its veil of water. It's still only a black lump, the size of a tractor tyre.

'Stingray,' says the Lamplighter. 'It's a fucken stingray.'

Gil and Keeley have dragged it into a few centimetres of water. They stand back and seem to be deciding how to untangle it. The Lamplighter doesn't budge from his spot on the beach. Candle makes a move towards his dad.

'Leave it, for God's sake,' yells his grandfather.

Both Gil and Keeley are still regarding the beached ray when Candle reaches them. They're saturated, and their faces are pink from the salt and the cold. The ray is immense. In Candle's imagination they are bottom dwellers that disappear in the sand on the seafloor, flat-bodied like flounder—but everything about the ray is enormous. Its eyes swivel in its fused brow, rolling to regard the men, and a gaping pit behind the eye closest to Candle claps open and shut, generating a noise he's never heard before, like a blast of wet air through a gun barrel. Its tail, as thick and as long as Candle's arm, thrashes through the air. He can't see any sting.

'Get away from it.' The Lamplighter has come up behind them 'Leave it there and it'll die on its own.'

'Don't kill it, Dad,' Candle pleads, immediately regretting the pitch of his voice.

'She's difficult to get in, wasn't she, Keeley,' says Gil.

'My word, she was,' replies Keeley, and then, 'Jess! Get out of it!'

Jess, who was cowering on the beach a moment ago, has bounded up, having achieved that state unique to dogs, somewhere between petrification and delight. She growls excitedly at the ray, darting dangerously close to its thrashing tail; she slaps her forequarters on the sand and woofs.

Keeley reaches for her. He picks her up and she licks his face.

'I better take her back,' he says.

'Yep, hold on to her,' says Gil. 'Candle, help me pull the net off this thing.'

The stingray isn't entangled. To release it, they only need to pull the mesh away from its body. The Lamplighter watches in silence as they gingerly peel away the net.

'Doesn't look like it'll get back underwater by itself, does it,' says Gil, dumping the net on the beach. 'Might as well give it a push.'

'Don't be an idiot, Gil,' growls the Lamplighter. 'You'll get stung, won't you.'

'I reckon the front end is safe.' Gil looks at Candle. A smirk glances across his face. He's going to try. Candle's heart jumps in his chest.

The Lamplighter is stomping back up the beach, away from them. Gil rolls up his sleeves and puts his hands on the temple of the giant ray. He pushes and it slides across the sand, across the film of water left by the last surge of the tide. He's face to face with it. Their brains are close together.

Candle steps closer to help.

'I'm all right, Candle. I've got her.'

The ray thrashes its tail against the sand, but its face, where Gil is, is sedate. It wears something like a tranquil frown. The opposing ends of its body seem to be ruled by different natures. Gil pushes the stingray further into the tide, hands pressed to its temple, and then his cheek to its temple. Waves gather around them, and Gil keeps pushing. The water deepens. The ray lifts in the water like a magic carpet. All of a sudden, with Gil waist deep in the sea, the ray surges forward. Gil stumbles backwards as the stingray swerves to the side, and sweeps into the ocean. The glistening hump of its back shows for a moment before it disappears from sight.

The General Store

Candle hands Kemp Tibald a grey sweaty parcel of fried chips.

'Boy, your granddad has been a keystone member of this community.'

'Thank you,' Candle says. 'That'll be three-forty, please.'

'Men like your grandfather are hard to come by nowadays.'

A newspaper slaps down on the counter.

'And your cigarettes, Mister Weatherly. That's eleven twenty-five.'

'I won't get a wink of sleep. What'll happen without your old pop out there—lighting those lamps!'

'That'll be seventy cents, Bianca. Shall I put it on your tab?'

'I still love him, you know,' says Sylla, filleting flounder in the kitchen sink before Candle left for work. 'I don't like you talking about him like that.'

———————

RIB COMES INTO THE SHOP, straight out of the ocean, wet sand still drying on his body. His eyes dart to his bread, his dates, tonic water, and linger a moment on the stand of rental videos. He chooses one, turns it over in his hands, before returning it to the shelf. With the counter between them, Candle can see tiny continents of sand still clinging to him, eroding; along his collarbone, the fair hair around his nipples, his belly button, the deepest part of his scar on his arm. Rib's bare body has had Candle interested in the names of muscles. Trapezius. Deltoid. Pectoralis major. Like names for constellations.

'Hi there,' Rib says. He didn't attend the town meeting the previous night, but he knows Candle did, and smiles smugly.

'Hi,' Candle says back. Rib's menthol cigarettes wait for him on the counter. A tender thing Candle can do for Rib.

'Oh, these? I'm giving up.' Rib grins, puts his hand over the cigarette packet and draws it towards the dates and the rest.

Candle takes a plastic bag from a hook at his hip and arranges Rib's things inside.

'Candle, come over. After you finish up here?'

'No, I can't tonight. I'm lamplighting.'

'Lucky Candle.' Rib rolls his eyes. 'The night, the flood, is black, is foul.'

'It is, it is,' calls Barbara Grig, emerging from out back, from the walk-in fridge, carrying a vat of batter. Barbara scowls, the lines on her brow forming a series of protective runes against Rib's bad magic. For Barb, Rib, the jumpship apprentice, is equivalent to a fallen angel.

'Oh, hello, Barb,' says Rib, opening his shoulders in greeting, puffing up his chest. 'You know.' Rib leans over the counter, closer to Candle. He speaks loud enough for Barb to hear: 'You know, one night he made me wade out into the bog to check a trap he'd laid. I let the crab loose and brought the cage back empty. Your granddad's a dick.'

Barb crashes a basket from the deep fryer into the sink and turns on the tap. Candle thinks he hears her say, 'Avaunt.'

'Come over tomorrow morning. We can have breakfast together. Go surfing?' A continent comes undone from Rib's clavicle. Sand spills onto the counter.

'Okay,' says Candle.

After Rib has gone, Candle collects the grains of sand into his hand, and brushes them into his pocket.

Stopbank

Ignis Xavier Gullstrand has lit the lamps for all of Candle's life, and much longer. He lives lagoonside in a house on stilts over a garden of potatoes and rhubarb, apple and crab apple, and dark bloody peaches. He hangs his clothes out to dry on the apple branches, and he bottles the fruit for Barb Grig to sell at the general store. The pole that he uses to light his lamps is propped against one stilt of the house.

The Lamplighter reads books on subjects Candle knows nothing about, like bear attacks, glasshouse assembly, gulags, and marine vulcanology. His treats are things beyond Candle's imagination, but Candle does know some of his comforts, like the cigarette smoke hanging below his ceiling, and the blankets piled on his furniture which still keep the fur of his dead dogs (Tiny, Ralph, and Ruby), and saucers of polished river stones and dulled sea shells that he collects from the beach.

Candle knows that inside the house on stilts, his grandfather, like every man who is in a house alone, is naked. Candle knows this, and he knocks at the porch, before going back down to wait under the apple trees. At the door, his grandfather changes his slippers for mud-caked boots. A stiff waterproofed coat is slung over his shoulders. Underneath he has put on a number of baggy cardigans, and thermal underwear, which he has tucked into his trousers; he has tucked these into two pairs of socks. He has swaddled the crown of his head in a bandana, and overtop fastened a black wide-brimmed hat. The hat goes on last before he leaves his house.

He descends each stair as if from a height. Hook-nosed and grey-maned. When he reaches the bottom he undoes his trousers and lets loose a bright beam of piss onto a stilt of the house. Afterwards, he climbs the stopbank, holding his lamplighting pole ahead of him. The wall of light he generates holds the swamp at bay, behind that brute bank of gravel, earth, and nightlight.

'HIS SKIN IS PITCH BLACK AND SLIMY, like the underside of a river stone,' begins the Lamplighter. 'Scabby with water lice and caddisfly larvae.'

He looks at Candle, strangely animated tonight. 'Like when you lift up a stone from the riverbed and the bugs all wriggle away from the light.' The Lamplighter looks right at Candle, to make sure he is forming that image in his head properly. In Candle's head he lifts the stone and turns it over, for him to see.

Candle grimaces. The Lamplighter laughs. Hur, hur, hur.

That laugh, thinks Candle. He pictures his granddad thumping on the back door, calling for Sylla. He pictures him ripping the crab from the dragnet.

That laugh, say the villagers, not looking Candle in the eyes, waiting for him to bag their groceries. Terrible, yet gentle.

He takes their coins, beams in tandem with the bleat of the till, and he looks right back at them. They know, as well as he does, that his grandfather is not gentle. But the villagers are getting worse. With the Lamplighter's retirement announced, people are getting wistful. Prematurely nostalgic.

Hwofff!

The first lamp of the evening. White fire fills the inside of the glass and the Lamplighter extracts the bright end of his pole. The lantern ticks and crackles as the flame within steadies itself. He unscrews the cap from a brown plastic bottle, the contents sizzling, and he sucks at it. He's already boozed. Another bottle slung at his hip contains kerosene for the lamps. The Lamplighter presses on, back along his path, and deeper into his favourite story.

'They call him Wet Pete and he's absolutely sodden,' he says, wiping his mouth. 'Putrefied like a bag of bad meat in the creek.' Gravel crunches underfoot to the same beat as his laugh. 'Drenched to the bloody bone!'

Across Saltwater Creek a swamp bird cries out. Candle pictures Pete there. He's crouching in the water. His oozing eyes are following their progress.

Ahead of them lies the body of the stopbank, its grassy flanks swirling, the trail on top bald and dry. The sun is disappearing behind the spiked back of Broken Tooth. The surface of the creek is turning to vapour.

Hwofff!

Another lamp fills.

An old spider, all eight eyes blind, sits unperturbed in her cobweb as the fresh light sears behind her silhouette. She has grown fat in this light, feeding on bedazzled moths.

She shifts in her bed, and waves her forelegs, as if saluting the Lamplighter.

He shoulders his pole.

'Do you know how you can tell if Wet Pete's been hanging around?' He draws shapes in space with his free hand. 'By his big mucky footprints, like puddles! When he comes to town he creeps through the ditches to cover his tracks.'

'Lots of puddles around at the moment, Granddad,' says Candle. 'After the rainy season.'

'Some poor old lady died the other night.' The Lamplighter ignores Candle, and gestures upriver. 'She dropped dead in her kitchen, with her hand clutched to her heart. Scared to death. They found puddles all along her patio.' The Lamplighter reaches up with his pole. 'Bloody Pete.'

Hwofff!

Another lamp, another spider.

'A few years back, Lorna Muller went for a stroll, to catch some sunshine, when she came across a picnic set up on the riverbank. It was a fancy spread,' says the Lamplighter. 'Buns with poppy seeds, warm buttery cheese, and a thermos of hot coffee. That day's newspaper still in its wrapper. A whole basket of untouched food, but not a sign of any picnickers.'

'Bloody Pete?' suggests Candle.

Hwofff!

'Merv and Waverly, from Bog Crescent, had a set of twins when they were first married. Little darlings they were, their names were Sweetheart and Hal. They used to go hunting for their treasures in the willow forest and bring back presents for their mum; things like birds' nests, and dead dragonflies, broken bits of pottery, and bunches of fennel. Hal gave me a big jar of tadpoles once.' The Lamplighter smacks his lips. 'Delicious!'

When Candle doesn't respond, the Lamplighter shakes his head, and takes a drink.

'That little man said he'd love to be a candle when he was grown up, like you are now. He was a good boy.'

'What happened, Granddad?' Candle already knows; the Lamplighter has told him many times before.

'A terrible thing. One afternoon Sweetheart and Hal went on a treasure hunt, but they didn't come home. The river was full. Those darlings will never turn up, people said. At least not until the river recedes. The day the search was called off a prize ram that'd gone missing did turn up.' The Lamplighter pauses. 'Well, certain parts of it did.'

Hwofff!

Since Candle was little, he has listened to these stories. Wet Pete was alpha in his grandfather's pantheon of made-up wetland inhabitants. The Lamplighter babysat Candle in his bed, while Sylla made lunch with Granna in the kitchen. Mean elephants, and meat-eating hermits, and evil-intentioned wetland ghosts would materialise on the riverbed, gathering under Pete's banner. But Pete outlasted his minions, persisting while they faded. Candle could tell, even then, Granddad believed in him. Pete was important.

In the autumn Waverly De Vol had asked Candle to tend her Amazonian sunken log aquarium, while she went on a trip up the coast with her husband Merv. Every second day, after feeding her school of stegosaurus-shaped fish, Candle had searched their cabinet tops and walls for some sign of the twins. But nothing about their home suggested Merv and Waverly had ever had children. What's more, Candle had never known fat Lorna Muller to go for strolls; she sat outside the general store, muttering to herself, and spitting on the steps.

The Lamplighter is radiant. There's a spark in his step. He looks sideways at Candle, to make sure he's listening,—

'Before Wet Pete got wet, he was a bushman.' The Lamplighter won't say more about the quality of Pete. When it comes to manful authenticity, only lamplighting trumps bushcraft. 'He lived most of the year in a hut over on Broken Tooth.'

The comatose volcano slumped on the horizon, dark green and spiked, like the back of a crocodile.

'The native name is lost, but the Maoris once held it sacred. They reckoned its peaks were liftoff points. The newly dead would flock there, to ascend to the afterlife.'

The Lamplighter throws his big shoulders up in an indifferent shrug, as if any mythology he is not author of is probably absurd.

'Pete was up on Broken Tooth, working. Collecting possum skins, maybe. Surveying for gold. Planting trees, or cutting them down. He was following a gully stream up the mountain, keeping out of the sun, wading and weaving around the big heavy stones that crowded in the rushing water. Tapped into some of them were strange drawings. Lines etched into the stone, saturated with an old bright pigment.'

Hwofff!

'They call them, those boulders, hag stones,' says the Lamplighter. 'Pan Ahn reckons he saw one floating downstream once, like a balloon. Full of heat, and air, and bad magic. Pete didn't know what the hag stones meant. He didn't know to be cautious. Following them he eventually found himself at a mountain lake, pooling at the base of a collapsed rock face. It was the source of the stream.

'Pete had never come across this spot before, and it was his business to know every inch of the mountain. It was not a spot you'd forget easily either. The lake was crystal clear and beautiful to look at. It was irresistible. Pete took off his clothes, and stepped in.'

Candle has heard Wet Pete's origin story many times before. In his head he has elaborated on this particular image a thousand times. *The naked bushman, dappled in sunlight. Water like silk wrapping around his calves, inching upward.*

'Something dazzled at Pete from below the surface,' interrupts his grandfather. 'Probably another drawing on a stone, Pete reckoned. He reached down and found a pretty little bone, the skull of a possum, or a feral cat. A thin fragile thing. He let himself sink down into the water.'

The skin of the surface sucked Pete in deeper, like the gentle, contracting muscles of a mouth. It crept up his stomach, chest, over his shoulders, neck, and then enveloped him entirely.

Hwofff!

'Submerged, Pete opened his eyes, and was astonished at how deep the lake was. The basin of water he was in slanted towards the rock face, and then plunged deep into the mountainside. It could've been bottomless, but there was a light there. White drawings dazzled all across the throat of the lake. Pete recalled a glyph from one of the hagstones, of a crooked snake body, tentacles, or arms, or heads, or mouths. He surfaced just as something moved up against him, breaking the surface a little as it slid past. Pete's legs were seized underwater, and held there, perfectly still. He had enough time to notice how the light wasn't touching the mountainside any more, but the tree canopy was lit up, and bright green. Below him the abyss moaned, rising to a tremendous mountain's bellow.'

Hwofff!

'When Pete woke up the sun was set,' says the Lamplighter, with some satisfaction. 'And the pool was bone dry. The rock face must've collapsed in on the throat, and the pool was emptied of that infinity of water. Not a drop was left, even the stream was less than a trickle. Pete on the other hand was soaking wet, a puddle forming where he lay.'

A greasy body of water seethes before the jaw of the floodgate, which is chain-tethered, and braced in concrete. Candle stands on the crossing looking down into the murk. His granddad is lighting his lamps, four of them here. They're halfway to the river bridge.

As it has grown darker the lamp fire seems less fierce, the flames globular, like egg yolks poaching in hot water. Below Candle, a school of herring swarms at the surface and he thinks he sees a bright yellow coil move amongst them. A sea snake. They come here on a rogue tropical current from the Americas. This part of the marsh is tidal, and salty enough for certain sea-born animals. Sharks frequent the lagoon, and have been known to try their luck up the inlets.

Candle turns away and looks out, opposite the swamp, over the reclaimed pastures. The different types of farm animals are kept separate in hedge-bordered fields, like figurines enclosed in fences of interlocking building blocks. There are the mares and a single wobbly foal, then a flock of coffee-coloured sheep, alongside a field of cross-eyed cows. A hare ambles fearlessly across the pasture in plain sight. Candle turns back to the swamp and glances down into the water, waiting for Pete to surface. His grandfather joins him. He looks down too, before sniffing and lumbering away. After a moment Candle follows.

'Pete didn't survive Broken Tooth,' says the Lamplighter, finishing his story. 'But his corpse wandered down here. My lamplight traps him in the marshes.'

The Lamplighter and Candle walk out onto the last stretch of the stopbank, towards the trivium and the river bridge.

The Lagoon

CANDLE LIES IN BED, the rain sizzling on the roof. The wet season was supposed to be over, but straggling rain clouds—stir-crazy and diminishing—were still drifting over Porbeagle, heading out to sea. Candle checks the digital clock on the cabinet beside his bed—it shows 3:02. If he gets up this early, he might wake his parents, who sleep in the room through the wall. Sylla always rouses as if from hibernation, red-eyed, one cerebral fold at a time, beginning with the most primordial. 'Candle,' Gil would call through Sylla's ursine groans. 'For pity's sake, get back to bed.'

The rain stops and Candle descends back into the underworld, shelf by shelf, until he is asleep.

When he wakes again it's 5am, and this time he's properly awake. He slithers out of bed, into slippers and dressing gown. Next door, Sylla moves in her sleep. Gil groans.

'It's raining, it's pouring,' murmurs Candle, a little incantation to tranquillise his parents. 'The old man is snoring,' he whispers.

He tiptoes into the lounge and dresses from clothes that have dried on the rack. He brushes his teeth. Outside it's becoming light, and through the sliding doors Candle sees a figure pass by, heading in the direction of the lagoon—it's Waverly De Vol, carrying a pail. Candle flicks open the lock and springs after her, barefoot.

'My angelfish become aggressive if they're not fed at least some live food,' explains Waverly, when Candle catches up with her. 'They're nibbling each others' fins, so I thought I'd find them something to eat in the tidal pools.' She holds up the pail for Candle to see inside—a little net, an eyedropper-like instrument for sucking stuff up, a booklet titled *Pond Life*.

'The booklet describes tiny creatures you can collect in the wild that are suitable for feeding pet fish,' says Waverly. Candle reaches for *Pond Life* and glances through the pages,—

'Artemia,' he reads out loud. 'Tubifex. Daphnia. Anopheles.'

'Not all planktonic life is suitable for the home aquaria,' continues Waverly. 'Sometimes something seemingly harmless can hide away in a corner, shed a skin or two, and change into something predatory.'

Ahead of them the boatsheds straddle the stopbank, dipping their sodden ramps into the shoreline ooze. Underneath, a storm drain empties fresh water and sediment into the lagoon, creating a series of brackish pools. The boatsheds will be shuttered and padlocked, each one cherishing a vessel. As they get closer Candle sees Emerald Tapuwai's glass-bottomed dinghy—boldly unprotected— tied under the ramp of her boathouse.

Candle goes ahead of Waverly, to the end of Emerald's ramp. The tide is in. Under several metres of seawater, tiny mud crabs, and some of the larger purple ones that live under rocks instead of in burrows, stalk about in the light of the new day. Waverly is looking out over the lagoon, maybe putting off her descent of the shingle bank, knee-deep into the overflowed pools. The sun is turning the sky pink as it rises. Every shelf of raincloud on the horizon has a different degree of saturation. The clouds are turning pleasant over the islands in the inner sea, having already spent their rain over Porbeagle.

'Shall I see what I can catch?' Candle returns the booklet to Waverly; she nods and hands him the pail.

Candle clambers down the stopbank, moving underneath Waverly as she steps onto the ramp. He's investigating the water's edge when he hears somebody announce their arrival, first by kicking up gravel, and then with words,—

'Red sky in the morning, fishermen take warning.'

Candle is concealed from view, but he can see the man in his black hat standing on the stopbank.

'Hail, Lamplighter,' says Waverly. 'But I wouldn't say red.'

'That's maritime red,' replies Candle's grandfather. 'It's what they call red on the open ocean.'

They all stay where they are. Waverly looking out over the lagoon, to the white ibis in the estuary, the greens and reds and blacks and golds of the swamp grasses. Candle hiding underneath her, the Lamplighter on dry land.

'Pity to see a person meeting their grief every morning on the swampbrink,' says the Lamplighter, eventually.

Waverly snorts.

'It is, isn't it, Lamplighter,' she replies. She laughs, not unkindly.

An ibis lift its head from the mud. It looks sideways at Waverly and croaks loudly.

'Such an unattractive sound from such a pretty throat,' remarks the Lamplighter.

'Your story,' begins Waverly. A board in the ramp creaks as she shifts to face the Lamplighter. 'The cne about my children, and your monster—'

The Lamplighter must like Waverly. He must like her slightness and bright, quiet eyes, thinks Candle. Candle can feel Waverly bristling against his grandfather.

'I've held the darkness from this village,' says the Lamplighter. 'My stories are good.'

'Your stories are the wrong stories,' says Waverly.

'He's out there, my dear. I can feel him moving, out there beyond my light.'

'Wet Pete, Lamplighter?' Waverly is facing the lagoon again. The pink is leaving the sky, it's turning grey. 'Sometimes things become darker, faster than they should. Without any help from monsters.'

Candle hears the Lamplighter moving away. His boots on the gravel.

After a moment by the water's edge, Candle emerges on all fours from underneath the boatshed. Waverly has wandered away, in the opposite direction of the Lamplighter, to where the shore becomes sandier, to where the few shallow salt pools meet the tussock, the dunes, and the shadow of the pine forest. Candle feels eyes on him. He glances around, expecting to see the old Lamplighter standing nearby, watching him. He's not there. There are no people around, other than Waverly. Candle stands up, shifts his hair from his face, and catches a movement further along the beach. Over a crest of dunes the tail end of something large and mammalian slinks into the pine forest. A stray.

At Bog Crescent, Candle stands staring into the yellow-tinged water of Waverly's aquarium.

The angelfish become animated when she switches on the overhead light. They've grown large since Waverly first brought them here inside a plastic blob of water. Their wafer-thin bodies slice through the grasses.

Waverly uses the eyedropper to transfer wriggling mosquito larvae from the pail into her aquarium. The angelfish churn at the surface in a carousel swarm.

Rib's Cottage

WHEN RIB ANSWERS THE DOOR he's wearing a sweatshirt that doesn't look like it belongs to him, and thin faded shorts, that could be swimming togs, or could be underwear.

'Come in,' Rib says, leading Candle into his kitchen. 'What've you got there?'

Candle has brought with him a paper bag of loose leaf Skull Cap and Chamomile tea. It's supposed to reduce tension. Good for people to drink when they're giving something up.

'Mum told me about it,' offers Candle. 'There's an information slip in the bag.'

Rib puts a pan of water on the stove and drops two slices of bread under the grill of his toast oven. He runs his fingers through his salt-bothered hair and takes the bag from Candle's hand.

'Thanks, Candle,' he says, flashing a smile. 'Shall we play a video game? We can surf later on.'

Rib lives in a cottage that sits at the very back of his aunt Emerald's garden. The two households are very much apart from one another, separated by explosions of bamboo, honeysuckle-laden arches, and a partially collapsed pergola. In his narrow sunroom Rib has set up a television and video game console on the floor. He has several game cartridges, but he almost always plays the same one. It's called *Return to Bones Beach*.

Rib opens a can of lychees into a bowl, spreads margarine and cuts the toast into fingers. He puts a can of coffee on the stovetop. His percolator is slow-working, so in the meantime he pours hot water from the pan into two cups, over spoonfuls of Sylla's tea. They take all of this into the sunroom and Rib turns on the television.

He crouches there, plugging in colour-coded pins, connecting the two machines. The TV flashes heliotrope purple, and then the title screen activates, showing a cobalt blue and yellow seaside, a tumble of pixellated waves breaking just below a banner in 8-bit cursive,—

BONES BEACH

'Here we go,' says Rib, taking a controller. 'Two-player?'

'I'll watch,' says Candle. Candle likes to watch the game unfold. The limits of a two-dimensional universe are lulling, satisfying in pace and predictability. He likes to keep a body count of the buffoonish enemies, and anticipate the mini-boss at the end of every level. He likes the cut-to segments, which show brief animations of the archenemy laughing, then despairing, then raging at the onslaught of the approaching hero.

Rib tips back onto a cream-coloured couch, patterned with blotted green foliage and pink camellias. Candle moves beside him.

'I see your granddad is retiring,' says Rib. 'Or, should I say, being put into retirement.' He pushes back his hair, tucking a piece behind his ear. The introductory story is playing in segments across the screen,—

Long ago, beneath the beautiful seashore sands, a secret was hidden . . .

'It's true,' says Candle.

'And they're not employing a replacement.'

'Nope.'

< PRESS START TO BEGIN >

The childlike avatar activates on a beach, spade at the ready. A blue crab advances. Rib leaps across the screen, following an arc of gold tokens suspended in mid air. He lands on the crab's back and it pops like a balloon.

'Who will light the swampbrink?'

Candle doesn't answer.

Onscreen, Rib bounces along a line of enemy crabs, eliminating a platoon. The room is filling up with sunlight.

'Who'll protect us from the swamp spirit?' Rib slams into a treasure chest, sending ten thousand points worth of gold bullion sparkling across the screen. 'Who will stop Wet Pete?' A red crab, which requires two hits to dispatch, lands a tackle, and Rib's health bar shrinks. 'Fuck!'

'Candle.' Rib is frowning. 'The doggod is the only thing out there worth being afraid of, and lamplight won't protect you from it.'

'Rib, is the doggod real?'

'Real as the scar on my arm.' He sits upright, and tosses Candle the controller. 'Play.'

Candle dodges a swooping puffin, and harpoons a charging red crab with the hero's trusty spade. Both missile and adversary vanish, cancelling each other out. Candle manages to stay alive until Rib returns.

'Hit pause,' he says. 'Look at these.'

Candle stops the game and moves in closer to Rib on the couch. He has a stack of photographs. A layer of dust coats the topmost picture, as if the stack has been sitting out, unwrapped. That first picture shows a crowd gathered in front of a pitched tent. A banner hanging above them reads,—

The Etheldreda & Fang Travelling Cirkus.

Everyone looks elated. A huge hairy man stands in the foreground with a smallish hippopotamus on a chain. The man has a big dark teardrop painted on each cheek.

'Me,' says Rib, leaving a fingerprint on the photograph. A younger, scar-free version of Rib sits upfront, cross-legged, holding an unlit torch—Rib was training to be a fire breather. 'That's the ringmaster Boris with the pygmy hippo. And they're the Balinese Bee Charmers. Those three are Hershey, Cosmo and Claudian. Clowns,' he adds.

Rib flips through the pictures. There are more clowns, with naked sun-freckled shoulders. A muscular woman brandishing a cutlass. A reclining goat. The hippo and Boris in a paddling pool. A lion behind bars, gnawing at a haunch of meat. Candle looks closer. The lion is wearing what looks like white face paint, haphazardly applied. Rib flips to the next picture.

'Look,' he says.

Candle sees two containers on the back of what could be a truck or a float. The containers have barred fronts—the cladding has been removed and propped against the trailer beneath. The interiors are in shadow but on the extreme left a panther has moved into the sun, up against the bars. A man in overalls is standing there with it, posing for the photographer.

'Do you see,' says Rib. He points to the other container, on the right.

Candle scans the black rectangle. Up against the bars in the corner there's something showing—a bushy tail. Something's curled up there.

'That's the doggod,' says Rib. 'See how the panther won't go near it?'

Candle sees.

'The night it got out Boris had set a curfew. He didn't often set them, so I should've taken it seriously. I think he let it loose. I think he wanted to get rid of it. He hated it. I'd snuck out to visit another trailer, but halfway there it called out to me, came at me, and grabbed me by the arm. It tore a piece off. It stopped for a moment—to chew and swallow. And then it took off.'

Rib is bathed in sunlight. His face glistens, he's sweating. Rib takes off his sweatshirt, one sleeve at a time, and then pulls it over his head. His bare body is so unlike Candle's. His skin a degree denser maybe, and with its own colour, not just blood and flesh showing through skin. He flops back down on the camellias and unpauses the game. A glare is on the television screen now, but Rib seems content to play the game by ear. Every line in his skin, every invisible hair on his body catches the sunlight. Gradually, if Candle squints, Rib becomes made only of these bright lines, except for his head, which leans back in a shadow. His thighs glow as they heat up. He's so still, like a body made of tea leaves at the bottom of a cup of hot, clear water. All the colour and tannins are momentarily contained within him.

The percolator begins making a sound, like a long, drawn-out sigh.

'I'll get it,' says Candle.

When he returns with the coffee, Rib has drawn a curtain and is battling a boss. A humanoid villain rides on top of a mammoth crab. He is withered and scowling and could be Wet Pete. Rib launches a spade, but the crab's shell absorbs the attack.

'Bullshit!'

Candle notices a clothes rack set up in the corner, partly behind the door. It's swamped with Rib's laundry, and several torches are propped up against it. Something half-obscured catches his eye in particular. A black and lacy garment. Lingerie. When he steps up to look closer he sees something else. A sequined dress is swept behind the crook of the door like a shed skin.

'Rib,' says Candle.

'Yeah?' Rib's mouth is slightly agape. A cigarette burns in an ashtray on the arm of the couch.

'Can you drive me to Anchorite tomorrow?' Candle asks. 'To see Granna?'

'Yeah, Candle,' he says. 'Sure thing.' Smoke rises from his mouth, like from a vent in a semi-dormant volcano.

Candle and Rib leave the cottage to check the waves. Emerald is hovering in the garden, with a champagne flute and a novel, looking for a spot in the sun.

'Hello, Aunty,' says Rib, finding his surfboard propped

against the side of the cottage. 'What a healthy way to start the day.'

'Rib.' Emerald speaks as if to both greet and dismiss her nephew in one breath. 'Don't listen to him, Candle,' she says. 'He knows it's only soda water. It's just that I prefer to drink from crystal.'

'Oh, I'm the same,' spills Candle. He's watching Emerald's speckled cat wading through the uncut grass. It glances at him. Its eyes beam weirdly, somehow multifaceted, like an insect's, or gemstones in an idol.

'Well, stop by any time for a refreshment,' says Emerald, smiling. 'Don't let that nephew of mine keep you cooped up in his pigpen all day.'

Rib has wandered away, heading towards the belt of pines that separate the village from the beach.

'Thanks,' says Candle. 'I'll do that.' He grabs the remaining surfboard and turns to chase after Rib.

'Oh, and Candle,' says Emerald. 'I'm taking your mother out for a row on the lagoon later. Why don't you join us? You can take the pedalo for a spin.'

Candle nods. 'Okay,' he says, then goes after Rib.

Emerald tips the contents of the flute in the garden. 'Come along, Whaea,' she says to the cat, and goes inside to pour herself a fresh glass.

Bones Beach

CANDLE TRAILS BEHIND RIB, along the spaces in between the dunes, where sun-whitened driftwood and tuatua shells jut from the sand, like bones surfacing from graves dug in a hurry. There are actual bones as well, picked-clean carcasses—terns, gulls, cod, rabbits. Pretty things when compared to the hefty contents of the old whalers' cauldron, which sits at the water's edge, on a concrete plinth.

Candle has been released from his apprenticeship, and, now that his lamplighting days are to be cut short, he feels like his anchor has come undone. It feels dangerous. He finds the great white shark tooth in his pocket. The surface of it cools his fingertips.

'Where was I yesterday?' Candle is speaking to the shark tooth.

'Entombed, under the sand, pending activation.' The tooth glows in his hand.

He runs to catch up with Rib, who has broken away from the dunes and is walking onto a curve of the beach. As Candle crosses the sand, picking his way through patches of dried-up bull kelp, he feels a sarcophagus move beneath him. The dark subterranean tomb he has been released from. It follows his progress like the shadow of a giant fish.

In the ocean, Candle and Rib lie bellies-down on their boards. They float just beyond where the waves are breaking. If they were to drop into the water between swells their toes might just touch the seabed. Every edgeless, enormous, shore-pointed ripple lifts them higher from the sandy bottom. For Candle, that unoccupied space beneath the swell is perfect—just sunlight, salt water, one of Rib's arms reaching towards the centre. Candle rests his ear against his surfboard, to listen through, into the sea.

'Don't get your head wet,' says Rib, looking over, sleep still showing in his eyes. 'Your flame will go out.'

Candle grins. When the next swell lifts him up, he tips from his board, bobs at the crest on the wave for a moment, and then disappears underwater.

Lagoon

FROM THE BOATHOUSE RAMP Candle watches his mother. Sylla is staring through the glass bottom of Emerald Tapuwai's dinghy. She pushes her pinhole glasses up her nose; a moment later she takes them off, swapping them for a pair of tortoiseshell sunglasses from her handbag. Sylla's willow branch feeler rests between her hip and the edge of the boat. Emerald has already settled down on the centre thwart, with an oar extending on each side.

'Here we go, honey,' says Emerald. She doesn't look at Sylla, her brow is furrowed, and she churns at the lagoon surface with the blade of each oar. 'The pedalo is just inside, ready to go,' she calls to Candle. 'Catch us up.'

The Porbeagle villagehead has braided her wine-coloured hair into a halo. She's wearing a woolly bush shirt as if it were a priestess's tunic—the necktie is undone and loose, showing the cleft of her enormous breasts. Her sleeves are rolled up, and muscles begin to show on her arms as she works the oars. She rows across the lagoon in the direction of the river mouth, leaving Candle behind. 'Try to avoid the kelp bed,' calls Emerald. 'The fronds will jam the propeller.'

With some effort, Candle guides the pedal boat down the ramp from the shed, towards the water. Its fibreglass hull squeals against the wet wood, as if in protest. He hops inside as it hits the water, and starts pushing at the pedals.

As he approaches the women, he hears Emerald say,—

'How's your poor old mum, Sylla?'

'She's good.' Candle watches his mother feign cheerfulness.

Emerald yawns like a lioness. She waits.

'She's as settled as she's going to get,' says Sylla. 'She misses the beach though—and the village.'

'Poor old Ellie,' says Emerald.

Candle spins the pedals of his craft, bumping the back of the dinghy. It's a deliberate move, to remind the two women he's there.

Candle's grandparents, the Lamplighter and Granna, are separated. It is no secret in Porbeagle that they had quarrelled and fought, sometimes fiercely. The Lamplighter needed to be hard, and it was to his wife's advantage that she harden up as well. Candle's mother, and his two aunts, have grown up in their parents' turbulence and heat, and eventually the younger girls, Wynell and Undine, rode that same hot current, up and away, to settle elsewhere. Only Sylla stayed in Porbeagle. She might have hoped her mum and dad would grow quieter together, as they grew older.

One night, on the onset of last year's wet season, Candle had answered a knock on the sliding doors. It was Granna, under the arm of Emerald. There was rain on Granna's face, and a fresh bruise as well.

'There's been a problem,' Emerald had said.

'Mum?' Sylla followed Candle to the doors, tentatively.

'I've spent all our money,' sobbed Granna. 'And your father's not happy.'

Candle couldn't imagine what Granna would spend a large sum of money on. Did she have a storage unit somewhere, full of antique clocks, beautiful furs, gleaming strands of real pearls? It turned out that Granna had attempted to soften the blow by suggesting an exchange of goods. Granna, Sylla said afterwards, was always skilful in the softening of blows—whereas the Lamplighter never was. While her husband was out lighting his lamps, Granna had taken stashes of money to the nearby watering hole, the Spruce & Spritz, where the barman welcomed her with shandies, the occasional gin and tonic, and silence— and the resident slot machines welcomed her with their honeyed lights and cheerful sounds.

Candle had sat with Granna that night. She wrapped up on the couch, listless in her cocoon of blankets, watching a game show on the television. She spoke softly, her eyes puffy with tears—yet Candle sensed something else besides her sadness, or running beneath it, barely hidden. It was an electricity. A showing of teeth. Granna was seething. Later that night the Lamplighter turned up at the back door, and almost broke it down—before he was calmed by Emerald and Gil, and led back to his house. Arrangements were made for Granna to stay in Anchorite, where she would be safe.

Leaving the lagoon, Emerald's strokes are steady and slow. Candle easily keeps up, pumping at the pedals, following just behind the stern. He sees Sylla take off her shoes, so she can press the souls of her feet to the cool glass of the boat bottom. She seems relaxed, but Candle knows she isn't always comfortable around the villagehead. Sylla has said before that she suspects her father and Emerald might once have been 'in cahoots'.

'The villagers gather behind your father,' Granna once

said to a much younger Sylla, 'and your father gathers behind Emerald Tapuwai.' Sylla told Candle she had appreciated the venom in her Granna's words back then, but only more recently had she deciphered the intended meaning.

In the dinghy Sylla is babbling softly to Emerald. Candle hears her say, '—for letting me know. About the thing in the paper.'

'I would have liked to let you know sooner,' says Emerald, and stops rowing. Candle pulls the pedalo alongside the dinghy, bracing the two vessels against each other. 'I hear Ignis paid you all a visit the other night,' says the villagehead, looking in Candle's direction.

'He'd been drinking,' answers Sylla.

'Your father is an emotional man.' Emerald balances the oars up on their hooks. 'It hasn't been easy for him, living a double life. A life warding off darkness on the swampbrink, and a life at home with his girls.'

Candle loves Sylla's sisters, his long-haired and laughing aunties. Wynell left Porbeagle as soon as she could, and moved to the tropics, where she paints portraits of tourists on white-sanded beaches. The youngest, Undine, is a tearoom waitress in Anchorite, and has a husband, a sheep-farmer, called Larry. Candle sees Undine every so often, and Wynell still sends postcards occasionally, with pictures of toucans and rows and rows of handwritten blither blather. Sylla is Granna and the Lamplighter's firstborn, and Candle often wonders what her life would have been like if she'd been born a boy.

The dinghy moves in the current. A herring jumps nearby, escaping the advance of an underwater predator.

'I think he would've liked a son,' says Sylla, to Emerald.

'He has Candle instead.'

Candle's ears prick. He looks up—and Sylla glances away.

'Hi,' he says.

Emerald narrows her eyes, smiles. 'It has been Candle's privilege; the whole village knows that.' Emerald can be astonishingly quick. She reaches over and takes something from Sylla, her willow branch.

'Feelers,' says Emerald, beginning something. She runs her fingers up and down the willow stick. 'Marvellous inventions. We humans take them for granted, don't you think, Candle?'

'Can I have it back, Emerald?' says Sylla.

'Well, I'll admit I'm thinking more of arms. With hands, with fingers. But feelers nonetheless. Our ancestors in the primordial soup started with feelers like this. Your mum's a throwback in that regard, isn't she Candle?'

Candle nods. Sylla is holding out her hand for the stick.

'There's nothing like being able to touch something, to be able to pick it up. It's the most intimate way of knowing a thing. Hands can be such gentle instruments.'

The sky has clouded over. Candle reaches over, bridging the pedalo and dinghy, and brushes his knuckle against Sylla's shoulder. He can see through the glass bottom— the sea is full of substrate and grit. Unanchored seaweed. Clots of algae bloom. They drift over a sunken sheet of corrugated iron.

'And then there are those of us without that capacity, without feelers,' says Emerald, sitting very still. 'Take the shark for instance. When a shark wants to touch something, to satisfy its curiosity, it has to use its teeth. Gentleness isn't something that comes easily to a shark. Just like your old dad, Sylla.'

A moment passes in silence. Emerald sighs, and holds out the willow branch, returning it. Releasing the oars from their hooks, Emerald knocks them back into the water. Candle pushes the pedalo away from the dinghy— and Emerald begins to row. He follows her as she moves lazily back to port.

Candle arrives at the boatshed ramp before Emerald, but is still hauling the pedalo from the lagoon when Sylla steps from the dinghy.

'You'll be at his retirement, won't you, Sylla?' says Emerald. 'You could pose for us?'

'Yes, okay.' Sylla turns to face Emerald. Candle watches. The villagehead is tying up her dinghy, one foot at sea, one on Porbeagle.

'Emerald,' says Sylla.

'Yes, honey?'

'The night, the flood, is black, is foul.'

'Oh, it can be, Sylla. It can be.'

The Hollow

Candle comes home from the lagoon, ahead of Sylla.

His dad is in the kitchen. He's just in from the garden and he sets down a colander on the bench. Inside several sprays of herbs are arranged amongst a crop of gooseberries. Every berry looks like a watermelon in miniature, the right size for a dollhouse fruit bowl, or a mouse. Candle pops one in his mouth.

'Are you making a pie, Dad?' The gooseberry splits between his teeth, squirting sour jelly across his tongue.

'I'm making a crumble,' says Gil. 'Don't eat any more.'

Gil's patience is at its thinnest after a day's beekeeping. His protective suit is slung over a kitchen table chair. It reeks of hot tin and woodsmoke.

'Where is your mum?' he asks.

'She was right behind me,' says Candle, who moves quicker than his cold-blooded mother. 'I guess she's gone by the creek.'

Gil turns the cold tap on, over the colander. He turns his back to Candle.

'You had better go back out and bring her home,' he says.

A FORCE OF CHILDREN, fresh from the school bus, plays along the swampbrink.

'Hail, Candle,' a bold one calls, ducking into the grasses where his friends are bobbing up and down like fox terriers.

On a good day Candle's grandfather would probably chuck them a line about Wet Pete. 'Pete's watching us right now,' he might say. Or, 'I missed a lamp last night. Hope Pete isn't waiting for you at your house.' Other days he'd blacken against their delight. 'Bugger off,' he'd say.

Candle isn't as confident in the same role. It doesn't feel that long ago he was playing with his friends here, with their same awe and fear of the Lamplighter.

'Oh, hail,' he tries, feeling his cheeks go a little red. 'Hope you don't drown in the creek.' He had tried for a nursery rhyme lilt, but it came out more menacing than he intended.

A small red-haired girl yelps and scampers away. Feelings of accomplishment and remorse briefly collide within Candle, before another kid cries out, 'Spider, spider!' and the remaining children scatter. Behind Candle, hanging on a nearly invisible strand, one of the Lamplighter's spiders has dropped from its lantern.

'Ah,' sighs Candle. 'Hail, spider.'

The lampposts lurk weirdly in the broad daylight. They're coated in pale green lichens and spent cobwebs. Some of them tilt slightly as if peering at their feet. Every lantern glass is filthy and, of course, without a flame. The Lamplighter is supposed to walk the swampbrink at dawn every morning to extinguish the lights, but it isn't often he does. They usually go out on their own. Candle steps from the bank down into the shade of the kanuka trees.

He slinks through the tree trunks to get to the walking track.

'If it isn't the Lamplighter's young man.' Someone speaks to Candle from the shade. 'The dead-end apprentice.'

There's a face at the water's edge. Peaked cheekbones and downward creases on both sides of the muzzle.

'My apologies, that was cruel of me to say.' The face has a body. He's wearing a high-vis vest. He has rolled up his pants and is dipping his feet. 'Calling you that—a dead-end apprentice.'

'It's all right,' says Candle. 'It's accurate.' He steps onto the dirt path that weaves through the trees along the creek bank. The man must be a council waywarden. Earlier, Candle saw a ute parked up at the floodgate, with the park ranger sigil on the door.

'Hah!' The Waywarden eases himself up from his spot by the water. He rises to his full height—he's very tall—and takes a step into the creek. He reaches down to shift something in the stream of water, the frame of a whitebait net.

'Any luck?' asks Candle. He has zero interest in the man's haul; the question isn't even a pleasantry in these parts, rather a social obligation.

'So-so.' The Waywarden is appropriately unforthcoming. 'I'm an acquaintance of a friend of yours,' he says, returning to shore. 'Emerald Tapuwai. She's told me all kinds of stories. Porbeagle's a funny kind of place, isn't it?'

The man moves in and out of the dappled sunlight.

'Yeah, I guess it is.' Candle gestures in the direction of the floodgate, where he saw the ute. 'What've you got going on here today, anyway?'

'Electric lights. At Emerald's petition, I believe. Should be some poles going up over the next few weeks.' The Waywarden makes an open fist and shakes it at his crotch. 'Hah!' He lowers his voice. 'Poles going up.'

Candle jolts at the man's innuendo. The Waywarden has monstrous proportions and is twice his age. Candle feels a tightening in his underpants.

'Ha-ha,' Candle says weakly. 'Well, bye.'

'Just one sec,' says the Waywarden. 'Poor kid. I've got a little something for you.' He moves to a hollow at the base of a large kanuka and reaches inside. 'Come here.'

Candle has been trained by the Lamplighter to never resist a summons. He approaches as the Waywarden produces a magazine from the tree hollow. He opens it out for Candle. The body on the page is reclined, legs splayed, a chest like a boiler and glossy thigh muscles. A cudgel balanced between his legs.

'Here,' says the Waywarden, flipping to the next page. Stowed in the centrefold is a ziplock coin pouch, with grey powder inside. 'Take it.'

Candle obeys. 'Is it—' he hesitates '—sherbet?'

'No.' The Waywarden grins. 'It isn't sweet, but if you put it in your mouth, it'll make you feel good.'

The stuff contained in the pouch looks like moon dirt. A handwritten label stuck to the side says *Black root, white flower*.

'Okay, thanks,' manages Candle, tucking the pouch in his pocket. He doesn't want to hang around.

'Don't mention it,' says the Waywarden, taking the magazine, and moving back to his spot by the creek. 'See you around, chicken.'

Relieved, Candle turns down the path. He moves swiftly around one bend, and then another. He still needs to find Sylla.

At Saltwater Creek

Candle finds Sylla.

Countless gnats swirl noiselessly above the creek surface; these mating swarms are also known as 'ghosts'. When the trout find them there, Sylla and Candle hear the sound of the water's skin being sucked away—and then there are ripples. Swallows collect the flies with much more showmanship, moving through the air as if the world—the creek, the wetland—belongs to no one better than them.

'Which is a better death for the fly,' says Sylla, 'in the belly of a bird, or the belly of a fish?'

The gnats sometimes connect midair, then spiral out of control. In the last light of dusk these living motes could be falling stars. Candle pretends he hears them sizzle when they hit the creek surface.

'They're beautiful, but things can look different in the swamp,' says Sylla. 'They're dancing the dance of love—and then they die.'

Candle knows better than to answer her. Sylla is speaking to herself.

———

CANDLE WALKS SYLLA HOME.

When they get there, a silky hen is inside, pecking at the kitchen floor. The gooseberry crumble is cooling under a fly net. Gil isn't around.

Candle draws the curtains, closing the lounge to the night, and Sylla coils into a beanbag on the floor. Candle puts on the kettle.

Stopbank

FOR THE LENGTH OF THE STOPBANK Candle has been paying attention to how he is walking. He suspects something about how he is holding his hips is giving him away. They definitely don't sway, but maybe he is walking too stiffly, or maybe he is stepping inwardly when he should be pointing his toes outwards. He tries that. It's hard to say. It doesn't feel natural.

The Lamplighter is way ahead of him, nearly at the end. Every blob of lamplight reveals his progress through the dark. Another lamp comes to life in the distance.

Hwofff, imagines Candle.

Anyone could find the Lamplighter. They'd only need to follow his lights to the river bridge.

Candle stops at a lamppost. It's a bit of a dud. It's throwing feeble flickering light down from the stopbank, onto a pond that has formed on the fringes of the willow forest. At the end of summer this pond will have shrunk. It'll be isolated from the wetland, a cut-off encampment of tadpoles and elvers and all kinds of aquatic insects. With the rainy season only just over, the pond's waters are touched by the edge of the river, which has surreptitiously crept through the willows. The river is like that, thinks Candle. A hungry amoeba, reabsorbing its offspring.

Gravel scatters. Somebody is approaching. Candle turns as two figures step into the lamplight.

'Hail, Candle.'

Seabright Durivage. Candle imagines pushing her into the pond. Does his apprenticeship afford him that privilege? Seabright's husband—squeezing, inching, pinching Romuald—slinks up beside her. A camera hangs on a strap around his neck.

'The night, the swamp,—' begin the husband and wife in unison.

'—is black, is foul,' finishes Candle.

Nobody speaks for a moment. Water slops against the bank.

'Is that your grandfather ahead?' ventures Seabright. Her bleach-blonde hairdo is luminous. Her milkbottle lenses reflect the flame in the lamp glass. 'We were hoping to photograph him walking the dark road.'

Romuald flashes his grey teeth. 'It's the end of an era,' he says. 'A picture might be worth a bit of money in a few years.'

Candle opens his mouth to answer. He would have said yes and pointed in the obvious direction, towards the river bridge. He would have lingered under the lamppost, letting the Durivages go ahead without him. Then he probably would've walked home.

Up ahead there is a brilliant flash, a hwofff louder than usual, and the shattering of glass. A lamp has exploded.

There are embers in the air. Romuald raises his camera— the picture won't come out.

'Candle, is your grandfather okay?' cries Seabright.

After a moment they see his silhouette staggering into the next closest pool of lamplight, and they all move to meet him. Candle isn't sure whether the Lamplighter will appreciate the attention. He can't think of what else to do, other than to go to him.

As they get nearer, Seabright mutters a word under her breath. 'Avaunt.' She's turning away a bad spirit.

Candle's grandfather says nothing as they approach, only quickens his pace a little.

'Hail, Lamplighter,' warbles Seabright.

All across his face are lacerations where the lamp glass has hit his skin. Each and every mark is leaking a trickle of blood, purple in the night.

Romuald catches up, with his camera in hand. He gasps. He points the camera and the flash lights up the Lamplighter's jigsawed face. There's a twinkling there. Residue glass.

The Lamplighter makes a sound. It starts as a gurgle and gets louder. His fists ball up, and he lunges at Romuald, swinging an arm like a wrecking ball. Seabright cries out. Romuald hits the gravel of the stopbank with a thud. Candle stays still.

The Lamplighter yanks the camera from its strap around Romuald's neck. It seems as if he might chuck it into the bog then, but he thinks better of it, and hurls it at Seabright instead.

'Keep it,' he growls, starting back along the swampbrink. Candle falls in behind. Even in his fury, his grandfather is a preservationist at heart, and can appreciate the story a photograph tells.

Granna's Flat

When Candle arrives Granna is talking on the telephone. She appears at the sliding door with the receiver held to her ear on her shoulder. Her cap of silver hair is messy, maybe a little wet. A seal's whiskers show up on her chin. She unlocks the latch and invites Candle inside. She continues her conversation,—

'Oh yes, Elmira. If he had breakfast, most of it would end up in the scrap bucket. Then he'd start drinking for the day. Yours?'

'Oh, well, mine would be into seven boxes a fortnight. Twenty-four per box, that's one hundred and sixty-eight, divided by two, divide that by seven. Twelve bottles of beer a day!'

'Yes, pickled is the word you're looking for, Elmira. Pickled. The same as mine.'

————————

THE STIPPLED CEILING OF GRANNA'S FLAT looks something like the surface of an ocean. The half-closed blinds and net curtains let the morning sun in and trap it there, filling the cool rooms with syrupy, befuddled light. The household items seem tentatively installed. A purple glass table lamp. A scratching post for a nonexistent cat. A television on mute. One of Sylla's vases, emerald and glistening, stands on the counter.

From her armchair Granna watches Candle. He's in the kitchenette fussing over a cup of tea, banging cupboard doors, hunting for the sugar he normally doesn't take. One of Granna's eyes, glaciated and blind, still follows the other in its trajectory. She sits in her armchair quietly, her feet sinking into the sand-coloured carpet. She looks relaxed but her hands are held in a tense diamond. Candle can tell she is about to tell him something. In his first memory of Granna, she's in the yellow bath. She blows bubbles through that same diamond of her hands held together. She softly blows into the diamond, her lips puckered in one exhalation, until she is whistling one note of music. Nine times out of ten the bubble fails, but if it survives the music is captured inside the bubble, and it floats out in front of Granna, towards him. When it pops Candle hears the single soft note evaporate.

He takes his tea and sits down in the chair next to her.

'Candle,' she says. 'When your mum told me you had awoken as a homosexual, well, I was concerned. I wanted you to be sure of what you were doing. But I never loved you any the less. Not like your granddad. He doesn't understand that you didn't have a choice in the matter.'

'I know, Granna.'

'I want you to be sure though, Candle,' continues Granna. 'I want you to be safe.'

'I know, Granna.' Candle sips at his tea. 'Thank you.'

'Here are some things. For your dress-ups.' Granna brightens. She hands Candle a cardboard chocolate box. When Candle opens it, he finds a tangle of junk jewellery.

'Oh, Granna, I don't—I'm not a—'

'Shhh.' She puts her finger up, as if to Candle's lips.

'My wedding ring will go to the girl in Undine's belly, of course,' she says. 'She's definitely having a girl.'

Candle investigates the contents of the box. Dulled brooches, clip-on earrings, fake pearls.

'Thanks, Granna. These are lovely.'

'I want you to have this.' She produces a folded kimono. She eases herself out of her chair, and opens it out between her and him. It's bright rust in colour. With wispy fish-like shapes and bare branches embroidered on the fabric.

Candle almost puts a hand to his mouth. It's very beautiful.

'I want you to have it. It was a wedding gift, but I've never worn it myself, and men can wear kimonos too, you know. Or you could hang it up on the wall, if you like.'

She hands it to Candle, who instinctively holds the heavy fabric against his body.

'I'd like to wear it,' he says.

'You'll look beautiful.' Granna is back in her seat. She fidgets. 'And, yes, men can look beautiful too,' she says.

Candle leans in to kiss her on the cheek.

'Oh, well, it's just a little something,' says Granna. She momentarily holds the tip of her tongue between her lips, like cats sometimes do. 'Now let's go to the café. I'd like one of those pink slices with the jelly crystals on top, and I'd kill for some scalding hot tea.'

They take a bus to Aquarama Aquarial Gardens on the outskirts of Anchorite.

The aquarium café is out front. A wheelchair ramp leads down into the main aquarium, past a mural of a strap-toothed whale and a wolftrap seadevil, neither of which are housed at Aquarama. Rib guides visitors through the complex. He dropped Candle at Granna's on the way to work this morning.

'Can we go in?' Candle can smell the otherness of the aquarium coming up the ramp, in hot waves.

'Another day,' says Granna. 'I'm hungry.'

A grimacing tiki at the café entrance recommends the chowder. Inside, a man in a dolphin-in-dungarees suit is taking his break. His dolphin head sits on the table in front of him like a centrepiece. He smiles and nods at Granna. 'Ahoy, ma'am,' he says.

'Ahoy, there,' she replies cheerfully.

At the service counter they order a pot of tea between them. Granna's slice is on the house. She chooses a table by the window.

'I couldn't hear a word she said,' says Granna, of the girl at the counter. 'I hate it when they don't speak up. It gets on my gate.'

Candle is almost certain the expression is 'it gets my goat'.

'Granna,' he asks, 'can you tell me about Wet Pete?'

'What about him?' She has extended her neck to peer out the window, but now she retracts it between her shoulder blades, like a turtle.

'Is he true?' asks Candle. 'Do you believe in him?'

Granna picks up her dessert fork and divides her pink-iced slice in two.

'Yes he is,' she says. 'And yes I do.'

The Library

'SWEET DREAMS,' SAYS CANDLE.

Granna settles under the top cover of her single bed. They're home, after catching the bus back from Aquarama. Granna needs her afternoon lie-down.

'Cheerio, love.'

Before Candle heads out the door he arranges the chocolate box and folded kimono in his backpack. He's meeting his parents after lunch, and they'll drive home to Porbeagle together, with a bootload of groceries. He has a couple of hours free before then. He leaves Granna's cul-de-sac on foot and starts in the direction of the library.

When Candle was a child the Anchorite library was much smaller. It had rooms more like a house. It had a decommissioned fireplace. That library was pulled down sometime between then and now, and a fresh library went up in its place. Only the red brick façade of the former structure still stands, facing the street like a stolen identity. The new building has supermarket high ceilings, and automatic doors. The shelves are all kitset aluminium and shoulder height.

Candle holds on to the shark tooth when he arrives. His eyes narrow, his lower lip juts out, he sniffs defiantly. Librarians are the kind of people who'll recognise who he is. 'The dead-end apprentice,' they'll whisper from the stacks. 'The disenfranchised prince of the swamp.'

Librarians are the kind of people who take an interest in bucolic tradition, in the arcane. So Candle imagines he has the propulsion of a thresher, and that he's gliding a metre above the carpet, pointed and honing-in. With his shark tooth in hand he's nearly a lamplighter.

Candle glides right past the children's section. On the subject of monsters, that's where the most colour is offered. The picture books are distilled, vivid, and recklessly self-assured. But today Candle is looking for something serious. He's looking for a particular book.

He finds it in the reference section. It's antique and seems barely handled. A pressed stem and seedpod have been painted gold, and inlaid into the soft red cover,—

BESTIARUM VOCABULUM
A MODERN COMPENDIUM OF BEASTS
BY
DIMITAR MEHLLER
AUTHOR OF
'BOTANICAL FOLKLORE OF THE WORLD'
'HALLUCINOGENS AND SHAMANISM' AND 'A LOVE OF THE OUTDOORS'

WITH EIGHT PLATES IN COLOUR, AND NUMEROUS ILLUSTRATIONS BY F. E. DU CANE, AND PHOTOGRAPHS FROM THE FIELD BY THE AUTHOR

LELAND, GREEN, AND CO.
39 HIGH STREET, HELLGRAMMITE
1947

Candle opens the book to the contents, and turns to D. He finds *Diamond—If a diamond is kept in the house, wolves cannot enter*, and further down, *Drac—A sea monster that can be repelled by burning feathers on the deck of a ship*. There's no entry for 'doggod'. Candle scans further through, and sees *Kynolykos—An enemy of man*. When he turns to that chapter there is only a brief description and no illustration.

In Ethiopia there is a predacious animal called Kynolykos (also: Crocotta or Dog-Wolf) with a remarkable talent. It is said to imitate the human voice, to call men by name at night, and to devour those who approach it.

The writing goes on to mention a Norwegian cartographer, a Torstein Svendsen, as having written of the Kynolykos before going missing somewhere on the Horn of Africa. Candle turns to the inside back cover of the book, where a pocket holds a yellow rectangular card. On the pocket a message reads: WOULD YOU LIKE TO KNOW MORE? ASK THE ARCHIVE. Candle slips out the card.

At the front desk he points to one of the reference numbers displayed on the card. The librarian, in velvet and tweed, types the number into the interface of the archive machine with the blunt tip of an acrylic nail. She caresses the dented plastic flank of the machine, and smirks sideways at Candle. Candle focuses his attention on the sounds the machine is making as it moves in its sleep. Somewhere inside a fan starts churning. It's reaching for the article, searching through all the fragmented and peripheral stories it must hold. After a moment the printer activates.

'There's no charge,' says the librarian, while they wait.

'The system isn't really working, so we'll be putting it out to pasture.'

'Oh,' says Candle. He feels a pang of sympathy.

A minute passes before the librarian hands over the printout. Candle mumbles thanks and leaves through the groaning doors. There's a park nearby, Queen's Garden. Candle finds shade under the rotunda, and begins to read the sample,—

From 'The Cult of the Dog-god'
Ref: 152-777-228
Parent: BESTIARUM VOCABULUM: A MODERN COMPENDIUM OF BEASTS

The animal, sometimes referred to as Kynolykos or crocotta or it-which-dwells-in-the-thicket, is the totem of a number of related yet unincorporated Quasi-Christian cults, the majority of which operate out of northeastern Afrika.

These groups are most often composed of civilised people who have dedicated themselves to pagan traditions, in particular animal worship. Torstein Svendsen, a cartographer from Oslo, wrote of his time with the ███████ ██ ██ ███████ ██████ sect in the Semien Mountains of Northern Ethiopia. His writings show particular interest in the Cult of the Doggod.

Despite the name, the doggod totems are not restricted to any particular species of canid. In fact the animal is depicted in religious drawings with a human face and a human phallus. It is speculated that these aspects might be achieved by shaving the hair around the face and genitals; these areas might also be tattooed.

The aforementioned sect look on domestication as a kind of sacrilege, and after a term in captivity, where a number of rites are performed around the doggod totem, it is let loose into the wild.

Svendsen writes, — 'It is believed that in the afterlife man becomes incorporate with God. Man's work, any physical evidence of his work in life, becomes holy, a religious relic. The domestication of the wolf is holy in this regard. It is Man's best work, turning the beast [i.e. the Devil] into a replica of himself, like God turning men into angels. Man works wolf into a demi-man, it becomes a sort of reproduction, — Dog is Wolf in Man's image. The animal [the Doggod] is reverse engineered by the ██████████ ██ ██ ████ ██████. They're trying to make the first wolf, so as to turn it loose on themselves. It is the Devil, you'd say, I suppose. At least the antithesis of God.'

Candle shifts the printout to his trouser pocket. He swings his legs from the bench, and gazes at his bare feet. According to both Rib and Svendsen, the doggod is a real thing. Rib says there's one living in the Porbeagle wetland—alongside Wet Pete, a drowned man, reanimated and turned dangerous. Both Granddad and Granna told him Wet Pete is real. Two monsters, then. Two stories brought to life. Candle feels uneasy. He needs to figure them out—so he can tell the stories right.

Candle meets Sylla at the spice shop. It's a narrow little place on the main street of Anchorite. The shelves along each wall hold vats of dried spices. Pads of funny cheese rest under fly-proof nets, and sea sponges and pumice stones hang on ropes at the counter. Sylla empties a jar of dried papaya into a brown paper bag.

The car is parked outside. Sylla and Candle wait for Gil to return from Anchorite's yellowed and squeaky-clean department store, where he's looking at fishing rods. Sylla is nipping and licking at the crystalline edges of a large piece of papaya when Candle sees her stiffen. Pan Ahn the crabber has appeared, moving haltingly along the footpath. The sun is on his lined and water beetle-brown skin. A look of serene emptiness plays across his face. Sylla hates Pan. Candle thinks part of the reason she misses the town meetings is to avoid seeing him.

'Creeping Jesus,' says Sylla, as he passes by. 'Fucking creep.'

When Gil approaches, moving at a slow and relaxed pace, Sylla starts the car herself, and honks the horn to hurry him along. She told Candle once, that when she was a girl, Pan would come over to her house to drink homebrew with the Lamplighter. Pan would kiss her and her sisters hello and goodbye on the mouth, and jab at their lips with his tongue.

On the drive home to Porbeagle they go past the fairgrounds. The night fair is happening tonight and it's already beginning to draw crowds.

'Should be a good haul tomorrow,' remarks Gil.

Sylla has her sunglasses on and doesn't look up. Her eyes must be hurting.

Gil's Burrow

They haven't been home long before Gil goes back out to spend some time in his shed. Sylla calls it his 'burrow', or, if she's in a teasing mood, the 'hiding place'. Candle knows she's interested though; he's seen her hovering under the branches of the pear tree, trying to peer through the murky window.

Gil keeps his collections inside—in sets of drawers and cupboards, on shelves installed in a hollowed-out grandfather clock, and in confused assemblies, strewn across his workbench. Some of Gil's treasures are beautiful; he has a wooden ruler that belonged to his father, with an inlaid ivory measure, and a concealed, removable blade for opening envelopes. He has a model of the HMS *Orpheus* in a bottle, a wallaby skin, and a tray of puffed-up purple and red scoria. A tiny ceramic otter went missing from Candle's bedside, and turned up in the shed. Gil didn't apologise. Instead he gave Candle the great white shark tooth in exchange.

'An old sea dog gave me that,' Gil said. 'I'm not sure where he picked it up from, but he spent most his life around the inner islands. A lot of seals in those parts, and a lot of sharks.'

Gil doesn't like to talk about the stories.

'There are worse things to be wary of,' he murmurs, from the kitchen bench. 'Things worth worrying about, besides talking dogs and swamp monsters.'

Candle watches Gil run a fingertip over a blister between the pad of his palm and his index finger. He sighs, and moves a steaming pot of peas from the stovetop element. He switches it off.

'It's bad people, Candle. Bad people will give you more of a hard time than anything from your granddad's stories.'

Occasionally, people did give Candle a hard time. Gareth Feering had once called out to Candle and Gil, when they were walking to buy ice creams from the shop.

'Everyone knows you're a faggot, Candle.'

Gil had grabbed Gareth by the neck, and thrown him to the ground. He could've found himself in trouble then, but Gareth's delinquency was locally renowned, and Gil was the Lamplighter's son-in-law, after all.

Gil ruffs up Candle's hair. Now that they are the same height, the gesture is a little clumsy. 'I'll be out in the shed,' he says.

Emerald's House

'ARE YOU HERE FOR THAT REFRESHMENT?'

Candle is making his way back through Emerald's garden from the cottage. He came to show Rib the printout from the library, and maybe to tell him about the Waywarden from the day before, but he isn't home.

'I'm all right, thanks,' says Candle.

'Nonsense.' Emerald is in a coral pink tracksuit. Her hair is in two plaits, one resting on each shoulder. 'It'd be my pleasure.'

She disappears inside.

'What will you have, dear?' Emerald calls. 'Shall I make you a lime cordial?' And then, 'Come inside. Don't hover in the doorway. I've invited you in.'

Emerald pours Candle a glass and guides him from the kitchen. Candle's home is airy and dim; the walls are clean and white. It's like living in the inner chamber of a conch shell. The interior of Emerald's house is very different. The walls are all painted in different shades—hot colours, terracotta, vermillion and sienna. The patterned carpets are turquoise and worn in places, and supermarket bromeliads stand in saucers of water along the windowsills, and on glass-topped coffee tables. Emerald keeps her house dimmed as well; her threadbare curtains are overlaid with pinned sarongs, tie-dyed and showing pictures of tropical fish and sea turtles.

'Take a seat, Candle,' says Emerald, leading him into a sitting room. 'I have something for you. I was going to wait for the retirement party, but now's as good a time as any. I won't be a minute.' She disappears deeper into the house. Candle hears a door open and close.

He sits back and breathes in the heat of the house. Has the man from the creek, the Waywarden, visited Emerald here? He said he was acquainted with her. Candle wonders if they're lovers. He pictures them in this painted cave, their bodies turning around together under layers of tie-dyed sarongs.

His hand finds the pouch of moon powder in his pocket. Almost involuntarily he undoes the seal and probes at the stuff with a finger. The particles feel as if they might squeak or fizzle if rubbed together. A curtain moves and the cat appears, jumping down from the windowsill. Startled, Candle brings his hand away from his pocket, too quickly, rapping the backs of his fingers against the wooden armrest of his chair. Candle brings his hand to his mouth to suck at the pain, but tastes the moon powder instead. It's bitter at first, then a little salty. The flavour is familiar, like the smell of hay. The cat, the speckled one from the garden, has pounced on a stack of something, concealed under another silk throw. The cat makes a single syllabic sound, less like a meow, more like chirrup.

'Whaea,' says Emerald, returning. 'Are you saying hello to Candle?'

The cat titters in answer, collapsing on whatever it has perched on top of.

Emerald takes the seat next to Candle and hands him a white gift box tied with a piece of thin black ribbon. As he takes it he feels something roll inside.

'I hope you like it,' says Emerald. 'It has a meaning.'

'Thanks,' says Candle. Pulling on an end of the ribbon, he searches for a better line. 'That's really thoughtful of you.'

'Go on, open it up.'

Candle shifts the loosened ribbon and lifts the lid. Inside, powdered with sand, there's a spheroid rock.

'Take it,' says Emerald. 'Look at it up close.'

Candle obeys. The rock is the size of a walnut and smooth to touch. As he looks closer he begins to perceive the segments that make up its shape. It looks like a wood louse rolled up, its head tucked under its tail end.

'It's a fossil trilobite from the primordial sea,' says Emerald. 'And you'll never guess where I found it. You'll have to move, Whaea.'

Emerald gets up and shoos the cat, who slinks down from her perch with exaggerated caution. Emerald lifts the silk.

Two stone slabs are stacked on top of each other. Two missionary stones, taken from the burial ground at the river mouth. The top one is missing a section, like a bite mark out of a fat homemade biscuit. The once living lichens have withered. Candle never knew for certain that the lichens were alive, until he sees them now dead.

'I've extracted a handful of fossils,' says Emerald. 'But that might be all for now. The gravestones are marvellous artefacts in their own right. The Historical Society will be interested, I think. Perhaps the museum will host an exhibition.'

Candle rolls his new talisman on his palm. The remains

of a prehistoric animal, taken from a stone, taken from a grave. The taste of the moon powder is still strong in his mouth.

'The trilobites were quite abundant once,' says Emerald. 'During the Palaeozoic era, I believe.'

'How amazing,' says Candle. He swallows. 'Thanks.'

'You could put it on a chain,' says Emerald. 'It's a piece of Porbeagle, to remember us by. There's a big world out there to explore, Candle. Have you ever been to the Inner Islands? To Hellgrammite?'

Candle is looking at the topmost missionary stone. There are the remains of a name there. A name he hasn't been called since he was eleven, since before he became apprentice to the Lamplighter.

'You don't want to stay in Porbeagle your whole life, do you?'

'No, I don't think so,' he says. 'I don't know.'

The stones hadn't been consumed by salt sea winds, or sunken in quicksand, or even tampered with by Wet Pete. Here they were, mined for fossils, maybe waiting to be sent to a museum, or to be kept here under silk throws in Emerald's sitting room, as her own private exhibition. Whaea rolls on the floor, sticking her feet in the air and stretching out her claws. Her eyes have become obsidian black, her nails are little hooks, kneading against the empty air, which is becoming semisolid, and too warm. It must be the moon powder.

'Thanks for this,' says Candle, getting up. 'And for the drink.' He finishes the glass in one gulp. 'I had better go get ready for Granddad.'

'Here,' says Emerald, handing him the gift box. 'Tuck

this away somewhere until after the retirement party. And I'll tell my nephew you stopped by.'

Candle nods. He finds his way back out of Emerald's house, crosses her garden, and walks back home. Inside his narrow white room, he lies in bed, trying to get some sleep before night sets in, and he has to join his grandfather on the swampbrink.

The Swampbrink

'Yes, that's right,' Gil is saying. His telephone voice is hesitant—he's speaking loudly. 'Yeah, Christmas Eve, at Porbeagle Hall.'

The ringing woke Candle up. It's still light outside. There's enough time to get something to eat before heading out. He joins Gil in the kitchen.

'I don't know about that, sorry. You'll have to ask him—'

Gil is interrupted by the caller. He runs a hand over the bristles on his chin.

'No, he doesn't really talk to me about that kind of thing. He keeps to himself mostly.'

'She won't be able to help you, I'm afraid.'

'No, not him either.'

Candle can see the patience leaving Gil like steam lifting from his ears and eyeballs—they are all turning pink. Gil turns to Candle. He startles, his eyes flash,—

'Listen, mate,' he says into the receiver. 'Get stuffed.'

Gil slams down the receiver.

———————

ON THE STOPBANK, Candle keeps close to his granddad.

He used to play a game with the lamplights. He'd pretend the dark spaces were devoid of oxygen, and hold his breath between every pool of light. He wouldn't activate his lungs until he stepped under the lamp glass—then he'd splutter and gasp for air. The Lamplighter had quickly grown weary of that game, and forbidden it. Tonight, for the first time in a long time, Candle feels a longing for the safety of every lit lamp. It's in the darker spots that the monsters will most likely strike.

Candle walks at the heels of his grandfather, peers into the blackness of the wetland, and tries to see into it, tries to make out what might be moving there. A bad thought crystallises in his brain. The lamplights aren't any help— they illuminate the border of the wetland, but blind the eyes against the deeper, darker parts.

Candle steps on the heel of his grandfather's boot.

'Watch it,' growls the Lamplighter, and swipes Candle around the ear. 'You little bugger.'

The Fairgrounds

It's not quite day yet. An ibis flock has alighted on the fairground. On the trampled earth they squabble over cheeseburger wrappers and muddied clots of candyfloss. In Egypt, there is a god of ibises, who is also a god of justice. At a threshold he reads the heart of a man, and weighs it. If the man has lived a virtuous life, he is given passage. If not, the heart is given as a piece of meat to the Devourer, a water-born creature that waits at his knee. Without a heart, the soul is without a seat, and becomes diminished. In this pitiful state it haunts the earth.

Candle once read about this in a book—*Mysteries of the Haunted World*—in the children's section of the library.

THE CAR IS FULL. Gil is driving. In the passenger seat next to him sits the Lamplighter, his face scabbed from the exploded lamp glass, the marks like so many seeds on a strawberry. Sylla and Candle are in the back with a metal detector between them. The dashboard clock says 5:43, but it runs quarter of an hour early. Last night the fair would have carried on into the early hours. There would have been fireworks, and musicians playing, and blankets held down on the ground with flasks of hot wine and packed dinners. The December fair draws big crowds. It always runs late into the night. The cleanup crew won't get going until ten in the morning, or maybe even eleven.

By the time they near Anchorite all of their breath has fogged up the windows and Candle can write his name in the condensation. He draws a starfish instead. Gil finds a back road that runs alongside the fairgrounds, hidden from view by a tall macrocarpa hedge. He pulls up and the car empties. They're all wearing coats with deep pockets. Sylla finds a gap in the hedge, and one by one they squeeze through. This is a family tradition.

On the other side the sun is on the grass. Everything is here that would have been in operation last night, except now everything is asleep. A comatose Ferris wheel, various vacated market stalls, caravans with pictures of hotdogs and cream freezes painted on the sides. The Etheldreda & Fang shantytown simmers in amongst the shearing sheds and stockyards. From somewhere one of the last remaining circus lions yawns itself awake and the sound is tremendous. The grounds are strewn with the remains of last night's festivities. The Lamplighter and his family are here to pick through them, looking for treasure.

Gil stands back so Ignis can have a go at the metal detector. Ignis found it at the dump, did it up, and gave it to Gil to keep. He kneels over the contraption, happily absorbed. Sylla and Candle move off together, to start searching.

'How was last night on the dark road?' Sylla removes her sunglasses. She's wearing a large straw sun hat that shields her sensitive eyes from the sun. She investigates the contents of a brown paper bag with her feeler. Nothing.

The Lamplighter had ended up lighting only every

second lamp. Candle had wondered if the wetland had become habituated to the lamplight, like a cow used to an electric fence.

'Same as bloody always,' says Candle.

Sylla sighs. 'Candle, I made you from leaf litter, and from your dad's honeycombs. And chicken feathers,' she adds.

'Mum,' groans Candle.

Sylla stops, she looks momentarily wounded—she begins again.

'Do you know how your granddad loves your father? Why and how?'

Candle has only a vague idea of why and how he loves Gil himself. Is it for the same reasons that Granddad does? Is there more than one way to love the same person?

'No, I don't know,' says Candle.

'I think it's because your dad behaves how your granddad thinks men ought to behave,' says Sylla. 'You know, your dad fishes and he hunts. He looks after you and me. He respects his elders. He doesn't talk rubbish, or much at all really. I think that's why.'

'And how?'

'Your granddad extends to him common courtesies, I suppose,' says Sylla. 'He shares his toys. He gives him his company, occasionally. That isn't something he parts with easily.'

'I should feel lucky then.'

'I don't think many people would envy you your grandfather, Candle.'

'Then why?' Something urgent and white hot comes alive in him. 'Why do we do this? This and everything else.' He feels the beginnings of tears fill the corners of his eyes.

Sylla looks at Candle. She looks away. Her big black pupils dart back to his face.

'Because love isn't always an easy thing,' says Sylla. She changes her mind. 'Because there is no reason.'

A low long beep signals that the metal detector is operational. Gil is a long way across the park. He calls out, 'Two dollars, love!' before the Lamplighter shushes him up. 'The gypsies, Gil! You'll attract the circus folk!'

Sylla waves and says, almost to herself, 'That's great. I wonder what I'll find.' She probes at a piece of litter. 'You know, Candle,' she says. 'You and I have hair the same colour. The same colour as bogwood and shipwrecks.'

'Yeah, it's lovely, Mum.'

Sylla's hair is long now; it falls right down her back, mermaid length. But Candle remembers when she shaved it all off. She had wept afterwards. Sylla didn't often cry out of grief.

The hour stretches on, into another hour. Gil and the Lamplighter sweep the grass with the metal detector. Their pockets fill up. Candle uses his eyes, and Sylla, her feeler. They pool their coins together. Beside a metal drum overflowing with rubbish Candle finds a twenty-dollar note folded in half. He opens it out for Sylla. The Queen's likeness, but green like a goblin, grins limply at her.

'You keep it,' says Sylla.

Candle moves away, drifting by himself through an arcade of unpeopled stalls. Outside one, two empty chairs sit facing one another. On one chair is a clearfile folder.

Inside are a series of pictures of different painted faces.

'Are you interested, babes?' A woman emerges from a tent flap at the back of the stall. She could be the Judi or Julie who once ran the shop. She has the same cloud-like perm. The same blue-tinted seeing-glasses. She has a steaming cup of something in her hand. A finger of steam draws a smudge on the nearest lens.

'I only have this,' says Candle. He holds out the goblin money.

'It's on the house,' says the Judi or Julie.

Candle flips through the book of faces. Each face has a name or a title. Longing. Recklessness. Sweetness. Darkness. Lightness of heart.

'Okay,' agrees Candle. 'I'll have this one please.'

He takes a seat when she offers it to him. The woman gets out her face paints and a series of small sponges and brushes. She smiles as she starts to paint.

When Candle meets back up with the rest of them, his dad says, 'Where've you been, mate?' and then, 'Jeez—Candle.'

'Your face,' says Sylla. She laughs. 'Who did that?'

'A woman at a stall.'

'You paid for that,' growls Ignis. 'Out of our money?'

'It was for free.'

'You look revolting. You look like a faggot.'

'Dad!' Sylla's voice is like a flame going out.

'Well, you are one, aren't you?' Ignis is going red. 'A faggot.'

'Enough!' Sylla takes a step towards the Lamplighter, into his shadow. 'Dad, enough!'

'Shut your trap, stupid bitch.'

Sylla's feeler activates. It makes a sound as it whips through the air. It stings her father on the side of his face, knocking out some residue glass.

'Sylla,' says Gil. He steps between his wife and his father-in-law, but not before Ignis snatches the feeler from her hand. He snaps it in two, chucks the pieces at Gil's feet, and gathers himself to his full height. All his parts assemble, stacking up, like a mountain face collapsing in reverse. When Gil doesn't budge, he wheels around and stalks off. As he leaves, it's as if the fairground is emptying. The lion yawns again.

'I'm going to Aquarama,' says Candle. 'I'll ride home with Rib.'

'Candle,' says Sylla.

The Lamplighter strides towards the hole in the hedge, and the car.

'It's okay, I want to.' Candle picks the pieces of Sylla's feeler from the grass and hands them to her. 'Bye,' he says.

Candle turns towards the real entrance to the fairground, far away from the gap in the macrocarpa hedge. On the way he passes through a flock of white ibis. Each bird, as it notices his approach, opens its wings and lazily lifts into the air.

The Aquarium

In the car park, a chicken-wire cover protects an otherwise neglected pond. Semiconscious carp look up, not at Candle. They're orange smudges in the green water. They don't mind Candle's painted face, ruined with sweat and dust from the walk here.

'Deepest desire,' says Candle, out loud. His desires are always so close to the surface. Semi-visible, like the fish.

Candle has paused at the pond to get his story straight. He's here to see Rib, but he's not sure if he'll be allowed to see him. He remembers the goblin money in his pocket—his entry fee, if they ask. He crunches across the car park. A rhododendron tree is in flower, and dropping its trumpet-shaped blooms on the gravel.

At the admissions desk, a woman stands with a tank of piranha behind her, and shelves of petrified bogwood, vacuum-wrapped in plastic. A miniature Christmas tree is plugged in and twinkling beside the till.

'Rib?' she says, turning an eye over Candle's face. She has a high, tight ponytail. 'Rib is working, he's leading a tour at the moment.' She narrows her eyes, trying to see through the face paint.

'Let him in, Jennifer,' says a muffled voice from inside a dolphin-in-dungarees suit. It grins from between two vats of half-price waterweed. 'He's Ellie's grandkid.'

Jennifer reaches up and pulls on her ponytail. Her face

tightens into a smile. 'All right, sure.' She holds out an ink stamp and Candle gives her his hand. 'Go on in,' she chimes.

Candle enters the aquarium. All the concrete is painted blue, except when it's white, and except for the tikis and the grey pillars of boulders that look like movie props. All the light wobbles as it passes through tanks, cylinders, and partitions of water. In the first chamber, large smooth pebbles lie under tangs and oscars and boxfish. They hover there, gills beating, nosing the glass. One or two to a tank. The filtering engines babble. Feet scuffle softly on the concrete floors.

Candle moves through to the second chamber—a tactile exhibit. Hands dabble in shallow pools where there are sea snails, sea anemones, and plump multi-armed sea stars. They're harmless, says a notice. Their venom sacs are removed. To Candle they look pummelled, bruised, finger-printed. He'd like to give them their venom back.

Down a passageway, observational windows look into a laboratory. A pool holds one giant pumping engine. There are more cylindrical tanks, some with lids fastened to the tops, others left open. Candle presses his face to the glass to see clusters of tiny animals move at the surface of one.

Around the next bend a conveyer belt pulls Candle through a threshold into a tunnel. All around him kelp fronds and the speckled bellies of wobbegong sharks coddle the transparent ceiling. He's moved through the tunnel to a stationary platform, and there's Rib ahead of him. In his Aquarama uniform he looks smaller. Older. There's no sunlight on him. He's wearing a little sailor's cap.

'Kelp holds on with a chicken foot. That's called a

holdfast,' says Rib, to a group of semiconscious visitors. But they're watching a John Dory.

Rib sees Candle. He winces—then winks.

'Hey, there,' he says. 'Care to join the tour?'

Rib leads the group back onto the conveyer belt and they glide along the last stretch of the underwater world. The final chamber of Aquarama becomes lighter. Candle can see rhododendron flowers through a window. Rib squeezes his shoulder.

'Hold on a sec, okay,' he says. 'I have to do the platypus talk. It's the last bit.'

Candle supposes this last chamber is meant to call to mind a mangrove. He investigates a series of tanks inlaid into a wall. In one, a single stone rests amongst an attractive garden of water plants. The stone is pocketed with holes. A plaque accompanies the exhibit, attached to the wall beside the tank.

ENDOLITH:
IT LIVES ENTIRELY WITHIN A SENSELESS BODY (A ROCK, OR A SHELL) AND EXPERIENCES ITS SURROUNDINGS BY EXTENDING A SINGLE EXPLORATIVE TENTACLE.

Granddad wouldn't stand for that. Candle can see him using a hammer to break open the rock. He would scoop out the animal inside—a collapsed jelly creature—and slice it into bite-sized pieces. He'd fry it up with butter and garlic.

Rib comes over. 'I get off at three. It's only eleven. Do you want to hang out here? Or in my van? Or in the café?'

'In your van.'

Rib tells Candle to meet him in the car park, so he retraces his steps through Aquarama, past Jennifer and the piranha, and back to the van. Candle's face itches where the paint has collected dust during the long walk from the fairgrounds. He picks a dried flake from the corner of his mouth. A few minutes later Rib appears with his arms full. He has his van keys, a can of lemonade, a wrapped sandwich, and a cardboard cup of chowder.

'You look tired,' says Rib, opening the passenger door. He places Candle's lunch on the front seat.

'I am. I was up early.'

'Hold still.' Rib wipes at Candle's face with a tea towel dampened with warm water. Candle keeps his eyes closed, and himself steadied on the side of the van.

'There, all clean,' says Rib. 'See you when I get off.'

Rib leaves. Candle sits in the passenger seat and eats his sandwich.

Sometime later, Rib nudges him awake.

'I got off early,' he says, grinning.

An aquarium cat, a fluffy squashed-faced tabby, is sleeping on Candle. He fed it his chowder before he fell asleep. It hisses lazily at Rib as he lifts it from Candle's lap and places it on the gravel.

'Avaunt,' Rib says to the cat.

Rib drives Candle home.

'Are you lighting lamps tonight?'

'I don't know. I don't want to.'

'Come out,' says Rib. 'Meet me in the shack. At eventide?'

Candle thinks back to the fairground—the Lamplighter breaking Sylla's feeler.

'Okay, I will,' he says to Rib.

The Shack

At the floodgate, where Saltwater Creek is stopped and
made sedate, the waters stretch out and form a convolution
of bogs and bulrushes. There is a network of tracks and
jetty-like walkways, leading to picnic tables on grassy
humps, hidden places in the sun, and one inexpertly
positioned whitebaiting hut, called 'the shack'. With the
wet season just spent, and the king tide in, the pathways
are underwater, enveloped by the swamp. Grasses steep in
yellow and brown liquid. Sub-aquatic rabbits graze where
they can, alongside spoon-billed wading birds. A tiny bird
with a red crown skips from one bulrush spike to the next.
The sun is setting.

FROM THE DARK OF THE SHACK Candle watches the
Lamplighter's progress along the swampbrink.

Hwofff—then hwofff—then hwofff.

Candle didn't let his grandfather know he wasn't joining
him; he just didn't show up. He has come out here instead.
In a pair of Gil's gumboots he wades along a sunken pathway
to reach the shack. While it's still light he checks for signs
of wildlife. White splashes of droppings underneath the
eaves. Egg sacs under rocks. Shed skins. Skeletons. The

window gaps are bordered up, the door swollen from the damp and wedged into its frame. There is only one room. Candle settles in to wait for Rib.

Outside, the Lamplighter has reached the floodgate. Candle watches him through a crack in the window boards. He's taking his time with the four lamps here, like he always does.

'Avaunt,' whispers Candle. 'Fuck off.' He wants him to leave so he can light a light in the dark room.

But after three of the four lamps are lit, the Lamplighter lays down his pole on the gravel. The last lamppost stands at the edge of the waterhole at the mouth of the floodgate. The Lamplighter lingers under it. Candle can still see him by the light of the other lamps. Candle watches as he lowers his coat to the ground. He kicks off his boots. Takes off his hat, and his cardigans. He drops his trousers. Now he's only in his thermal underwear and the bandana swaddling his crown. His grey mane sticks out in places.

In his dark room Candle thinks he shouldn't want to watch. He does though. He wants to see what the Lamplighter will do. Is he going to drown himself? Will Candle have to try to save him? He wants to see the Lamplighter's bare body. He has never posed at a town meeting. Candle imagines tallow-like flesh melted on a bony frame. And underneath that a hot heart must beat. Hur—hur—hur. Like an endolithic jelly.

The Lamplighter sheds his undergarments. His body is like Candle imagined, but less so. He replaces his black hat, screwing it onto his skull.

Candle watches as the old man gingerly moves to the water's edge, and, in an animal kind of way, collapses his body with a splash and a faint gasp. He is out of sight now, but Candle can picture the black hat at the water surface. He can picture a thousand tiny fish nibbling the dead skin from the Lamplighter's body, and sharks steering away, adjusting their territorial borders.

It's not long before the Lamplighter rises out from the floodgate, swamp water falling from him, as if from Wet Pete himself. He takes off his hat and shakes off the water. He returns his clothes to his body, and then his boots, and then replaces his hat. He leaves along the stopbank. It's as if he was never there at all.

Candle has a head torch with him. He turns it on and is momentarily blinded. There is a broken mirror in the shack. The bulb in the head torch pulses weakly, the battery low. He turns it off. Back in the dark a long moment passes, perhaps many minutes, before Candle startles.

'What is it?' Candle is talking to himself, but the doggod answers from outside the shack,—

'C'mon, Candle,' it says. 'Somebody's in the grasses.'

Candle's skin freezes in the dark room. He checks the gap in the window. Nothing. It's dark outside, darker with one less lamp at the floodgate. Right before his eyes another lamp extinguishes. His view is suddenly blocked. Jaws snap at the window boards.

'No wolves in this country,' barks a voice, not unlike the Lamplighter's.

'Rib says there are.' Candle knows enough to keep monsters talking.

'There are,' it says. 'Hundreds.'

Candle can hear it scrambling around the perimeter of the shack, checking for any weaknesses, any entry points.

When it comes to the door it rakes at the damp wood with its claws.

'Avaunt,' says Candle.

'Hah,' it responds. 'Fuck off.'

'Avaunt,' repeats Candle. 'The Lamplighter's at the bridge. Try your luck with him.'

'The bridge,' barks the voice. It makes a noise, an indecipherable composite sound, part human and part animal. 'Porbeagle will go to the dogs, without your granddad.' It rakes at the door. Something flashes at the bottom, and then pulls away. A paw? Candle can hear it panting, clearing its throat, as it circles the shack again. He checks the window just as it comes into view. It's bigger than an Alsatian, smaller than a mare. Its eyes catch some light; they're the same colour as the star Antares.

Candle feels in his coat for his talismans. He slips on the citrine and silver ring, but it's not a diamond. He touches the bag of moon powder. Emerald's fossil. And then something thin and soft brushes against his hand—the hawk feather. Candle keeps a cigarette lighter in his pants pocket. He uses it to set the beautiful barred feather alight. It catches fire, producing a pungent coil of smoke. A section of wood breaks away at the bottom of the door. Big enough for a rat to squeeze through. A muzzle appears there. Its nostrils flare. It smells the smoke.

'Come,' it says. 'Come to me.' It pushes its nose through. Its lips snarl, showing a set of long canines.

The tooth! Candle scrambles in his pocket. He feels a piece of cold crystal smoke in his hand. He swoops, slashing at the doggod's muzzle. There's a yelp and it retracts.

The doggod moans, an eerie wailing sound. Candle

listens as it crashes into the bulrushes. He shrinks into the far corner of the shack, and wipes the blood from his most powerful talisman. He feels electric; his heart thumps in his chest. Candle doesn't move until, some time later, a light shines on the shack. It shines through all the cracks in the walls.

'Come out, Candle,' someone calls. It's Rib.

Candle kicks the stuck door from its frame, breaking free from the shack. Rib is in the water, standing alongside his aunt's glass-bottomed dinghy. The doggod could still be close by, licking its wound—waiting. The scar on Rib's bare arm glistens. He turns and sees Candle at the door of the shack.

'Come on, Candle,' says Rib.

The bulrushes move alongside the shack.

'Rib,' calls Candle, but it comes out a whisper. His heart seizes. 'Get back!'

The doggod emerges from the rushes, the whites of its teeth and eyes bright. Its muzzle bloody.

'Come to me,' calls the doggod. Candle understands what it must have been like that night at the circus. No walls separate Rib from the animal. It's growling, the sound is like a trap being wound up. It springs forward, its jaws open wide.

Hwofff.

Rib activates a link, a torch made from pitch and flax bundled together, and it combusts. A fireball balloons up from Rib's mouth, and the swamp lights up—thousands of flying insects are revealed, floating above the grasses. The doggod howls, a sound entirely animal, and retreats back into the wetland. The flame goes out, and it's dark again.

'Care for a ride?' calls the fire breather. Rib's voice is shaking.

Candle wades out to meet Rib, and they both climb into the boat together without speaking. There are several blankets piled on the bottom.

'Candle, are you all right?' asks Rib. 'You were here by yourself. Did it call out to you?'

'Yes,' says Candle, taking off his gumboots and stowing them at the bow. 'I saw my granddad. After he left, the doggod tried to get inside.'

'Fuck, Candle! Are you okay?'

'I'm okay. I'm almost a lamplighter.'

Rib frowns. 'Almost.'

Candle leans towards him. He stumbles, grazing his bottom lip against Rib's cheek, before kissing him on the side of the mouth.

Rib drops the ends of the oars in the water.

'Candle—'

'We should get away from here.'

Rib stares a long moment, before lifting the oars. He smiles and begins to row down Saltwater Creek towards the lagoon.

After they're gone the Lamplighter comes trudging back through the dark. The lamps have all gone out over the floodgate. At the crossing he stops and stares down into the water.

The Ocean

In Emerald Tapuwai's glass-bottomed dinghy, Rib rows Candle from the floodgate, down Saltwater Creek, and out into the lagoon. He doesn't stop: he rows across the lagoon surface, past the boatsheds, past a flock of sleeping ibis, each one balancing on one leg in the mud. From the lagoon he joins the greater river. He barely has to work now; the current takes them to the mouth.

Out on the open ocean they can see cruise ships twinkling pinkly as they move in their sleep between the island resorts.

Candle once found a piece of red sea glass on the beach. Sea glass in itself isn't rare. He could fill his pockets after one shoreline sweep. Tellingly, the most common colours to be found were the amber-browns and algal-greens of beer bottles. The red sea glass, Candle had thought, was a special find.

'You keep it.' Sylla keeps an old lantern on the dinner table full of sea glass. She doesn't like the colour red.

'Where did it come from, Mum?' Candle had asked.

'How am I supposed to know?'

'Do you think it's from something, like a red window?'

'No one will ever be able to tell you where that piece of sea glass came from, Candle.'

He made a face at Sylla's venom.

'Oh, it's probably from a cruise ship,' she said, retracting her fangs. 'Like all the rubbish washed up here. Rubbish from those cruise ships.'

'Oh, ship glass.'

The surface of the ocean shivers all around Candle and Rib, even though the air is warm. As they near a cruise ship, one of its great glass eyes seems to roll towards them, to regard the castaway humans in their dinghy.

'Candle,' says Rib. They're sitting opposite one another and their knees touch first.

Candle shrugs off his coat and moves to Rib's side, wobbling the boat on the ocean beneath them. Rib reaches to steady Candle. His hand slips underneath the bottom hem of Candle's T-shirt, glancing across the flank of his belly, gripping his hipbone. This is enough. They kiss. Candle's mouth becomes something it wasn't before. A muscle-instinct materialises. His hands activate and find Rib's body. Rib moves a woollen blanket, clumsily spreading it out on the boat bottom.

From the ocean depths a school of ovaloid jellies pause underneath the dinghy. As they hang in the water their bodies ripple with phosphorescence. The colours shift from electric pink, to scarlet, to a dull, dark amethyst.

Rib lies back, and lifts his hips, wriggling out of his shorts. His underpants are purplish-red—a light at the small of Candle's back pulses, and he wonders if he has synesthesia. Rib finds Candle's hands and helps him unpeel the underwear from his hips. Rib's erection rebounds on the plain below his navel.

'Candle,' says Rib. 'Take off your clothes.'

Underneath the dinghy the school shifts formation, spreading out. Each jelly contracts, and then dilates, undulating to hold their positions in the water. Their lights intensify. They turn bright pink and hold the colour. The dinghy rocks in the water and the glowing creatures disband. One by one they turn off their lights and sink back into the deep sea.

Porbeagle Row

Candle is walking home from Rib's.

Only the waders are awake—and Waverly De Vol, who raises her hand in greeting from a distance. The ibises croak and plunge their bills into the mud, fishing for sea worms and baby fish. Candle goes home by way of the Lamplighter's apple tree garden—this feels cavalier, dangerous. He's sleeping up there, up in the house on stilts.

Sylla and Gil are always asleep in bed before Candle returns home from lamplighting. They're both surprised to see him come in through the sliding doors, fully dressed.

'Where've you been, Candle?' Sylla is in her fluffy dressing gown. She's holding a coffee can full of chicken feed. Gil is already in the lower larger piece of his beekeeping suit.

'I stayed the night at Rib's.'

Sylla frowns.

'Candle—'

'It's nothing. We took Emerald's boat out last night.'

'You stole her boat?'

'We didn't steal it. We gave it back.' Candle approaches Sylla, handing her a long piece of willow he picked up from the beach on the way home. It needs buffing up, but it has a nice shape to it, twisted slightly, like a liquorice coil.

'Thanks, love,' says Sylla, and her eyes fill up with tears. 'I'm sorry about what happened yesterday. I don't think you should go out with your grandfather anymore.'

'We'll see,' says Candle. He lets Sylla kiss him on the cheek. 'I think I should see my apprenticeship through to the end. It's not too far away.'

Sylla sniffs, and nods. She shuffles outside to feed her hens, taking her new feeler with her.

'Good boy,' says Gil, smacking Candle's head with a kiss. 'You shouldn't have taken Emerald's boat though,' he says, smiling. 'If that old dragon finds out you'll both be in trouble. You and Ribby.' He laughs. 'Hey, Candle. Did you see my new queen?'

Gil hands Candle a plastic container, a little larger than a matchbox, but narrower. It contains two chambers, one with a clear plastic window, and one with a window of gauze. Behind the gauze a queen bee hums a single note. Candle can feel it through his thumb and fingertip.

'Be careful. She has a sting.'

Gil leaves for work. Sylla stays with her chickens, picking weeds out of the garden. Candle has nowhere to go, nothing to do. His heart feels like a hoop, with something jumping through it. A circus seal? An aquarium cat?

But there was something else. Something about last night was bothering him. It was the swim the Lamplighter had taken. He had gone in so fearlessly. Wasn't he afraid of what he might meet in the water below the floodgate?

At dinner, Candle asks Sylla, 'What was it that Granddad did, before he became a lamplighter?'

'He was a candle like you of course,' she says. 'But he did spend some time up on Broken Tooth. Your grandmother says he used to love exploring the bush. He'd spend whole weekends away with his mates, hunting and fishing.'

No wonder Wet Pete's origin story was one of Granddad's favourites. Candle is suddenly aware of the limits put on his grandfather's life when he took up the mantle of Lamplighter. He feels a little sad.

'Granna called,' says Sylla. 'She'd like to see you tomorrow.'

'I'll catch a ride in with Rib.'

Sylla ladles some sea-lily stew into Gil's emptied bowl. 'I could drive you. My eyes are getting better. I can wear my sunglasses.'

'Thanks, but it's okay, Mum.'

'Candle, come for a walk to the beach after dinner,' says Gil. 'Your mum will come too, won't you, love?'

Candle sees Sylla at the sink. She starts the tap, releasing a gush of water on the empty stew pan.

'Yes, I'll bring the camera,' she says. 'Will you take some pictures, Candle?'

It's dark outside. Sylla has cooked late. Candle pushes back his chair.

'Yeah, sure,' he replies. 'That'll be nice.'

Bones Beach

SYLLA AND GIL ON THE BEACH AT NIGHT,—

The camera flash illuminates their faces; Sylla clinging to Gil; her driftwood-coloured complexion; laughing, flashing her eyeeth, foam-white and pointed.

Candle hasn't worn shoes. In the dark he walks away from his parents, towards the sound of waves, until the sand grows damp underfoot. The edge of the ocean reaches to touch his feet, and then slinks back. He lifts the camera and the flash rebounds on the ocean surface. Candle knows the pictures won't come out.

When he moves back onto land, back towards his parents, Gil bellows and lifts Sylla into the air. She calls to Candle, laughing and calling his name in the dark.

'Save me, Candle,' she laughs. 'It's Wet Pete.'

Candle runs over and grabs one of her legs. He pulls until Gil releases his grip. Sylla and Candle collapse into the sand, Sylla is giddy and still laughing. Candle is silent.

At Granna's flat

GRANNA HAS NO OTHER GRANDCHILDREN, but she still keeps a wicker crate of second-hand toys and colouring books in her sitting room. Candle finds a clean page in one, and plays dot-to-dot. It's a kitten playing the trombone.

Granna moves about in her kitchenette. They had canned soup for lunch, and she's rinsing the dishes. The electric jug is whistling. When she moves back into the room she has a cup of tea in each hand.

'It's green, Candle,' she says. 'It'll settle your gizzard.'

Granna eases herself into her chair. She picks up her new toy from the tea table, a Tetris-like console she ordered from a catalogue. Its called a Pocket Hermann. It generates pixellated inkblots.

'What do you see?' asks Granna.

Candle studies the screen. 'A stingray,' he says.

'Yes, good.' Granna presses a button on the console and the pixels shift. She shows it to Candle.

'Another stingray, between two men facing each other.'

'Next one.' Granna presses the button again.

'A crab. Looking at a butterfly.'

And again. And six more times after.

A face. A sand spider. A wallaby skin. Two open eyes, and an open mouth. An empty lantern. A flame in the shape of a heart. The contents of a rock pool.

'Good boy,' says Granna. She sets the console aside and

gently takes his hand. Candle wasn't expecting her to. Her nails are polished, her skin is like soft quartz. She presses a crinkled green note into Candle's hand. Twenty more goblin dollars. Now he has forty.

'I used to walk with him lighting his lamps,' Granna tells Candle, as if she paid him so she could begin. 'When he and I were first married, I would walk the dark road with him, out beyond the limits of the village.'

At her bedside Sylla keeps a framed black-and-white photograph of Granna as a young woman. The photographer is looking down on her as she moves across the surface of the lagoon, through water like milk, her cleavage buoyant, and dark hair slicked back. Her brow is solemn, yet there's laughter in her eyes, or cunning.

Barracuda, the Lamplighter would call her sometimes.

Granddad's picture is on the wall. A clean-shaven young man leaning in the doorway of his father's shed, hands in his pockets, smirking shyly.

'He used to say that every man in the village would give anything to have his job.' Granna rolls her good eye, and the other one obediently follows. 'He always boasted about his fine quality. He wanted to convince me I'd got a good deal marrying him,' she says.

Granna reaches for something beside her armchair. Two or three TV guides slide from the family bible. It's thicker than a stack of phonebooks, and the front cover is inlaid with golden vines. Granna lifts it to her lap, and begins to search the pages.

The bible is a container. Candle had once asked to borrow it for a photography assignment in high school, sure that its weight—its supposed family significance—

would in itself generate great photographs and improve his marks. All through the pages Granna has filed an array of documents, some significant, some of questionable significance. Newspaper birth announcements, wedding invitations (Candle's parents!), a fortune from a fortune cookie: 'no answer is also an answer', a table of runes, and an orphaned tarot card, The Hermit. Candle once found a page torn from a women's magazine. He hadn't been able to guess which side of it was for keeping—the recipe for asparagus roulade, or the first page of a story, a film star confessional.

As Granna leafs through, a prayer card detaches and falls, circling like a sycamore seed to the carpet. Candle picks it up. The picture shows the archangel Michael— rose-fleshed and clad in golden armour—crushing Lucifer under his feet, his sword hovering above the Devil's frog-coloured breast. Hellfire pools there, enveloping Michael's feet. The flames look tender somehow.

'Here it is,' says Granna, after a moment. She lifts a scrap of paper to her chest. It's a newspaper clipping. She closes the bible and places the clipping facedown on top.

'My love,' she says. 'I love you.' She shifts in her seat. 'I'm sorry to show you this.'

Granna hands Candle the clipping.

'He told me a story when we were newly married,' she says. 'Him and Pan would hide down by the bridge. Down where the men from the city would go to meet, to light fires. Down where the wild clematis grows.'

The newspaper article is headed BODY FOUND IN THE FLOOD. The picture of the young man looks like it was taken at the morgue. It shows his face. He has two black eyes and there is blood around his nostrils.

Hur—hur—hur. Candle's heart throbs.

'Your granddad was beautiful back then, and he'd call out to them,' says Granna. 'He'd choose a man, and call him out from under the bridge, then lead him away to a quiet spot in the willow forest, where Pan was waiting. He told me that, once they'd got one of these guys alone, they'd knock him around a bit. Give him a fright. He told me this like it was something to be proud of. Like he was showing me his good quality.'

The boy in the picture has a silver ring in his ear.

'I was appalled,' says Granna. 'I told him that was a disgusting thing for him to do. He shut up about it then. I thought that was that.'

Candle tries to read. The article describes the boy as a man from the city, and a deviant. Candle's heartbeat is making his head wobble. His eyes won't concentrate on the words. 'Lewd behaviour under the bridge,' says the article, with distaste.

'Our paper didn't print a follow-up when the body was identified, but Hellgrammite did.' Granna hands Candle another clipping, which he takes without looking up. 'His name was Peter,' she says. 'He must've been disorientated afterwards. He ran away from them and fell off the floodgate. Ignis hadn't lit the lamps.' Candle looks up at her. A tear rolls from her good eye down her cheek, her bad eye releases another, a moment later. 'I sent his mother a condolence card.'

DROWNED MAN IDENTIFIED:—The body recovered from the Porbeagle River wetland on April 28th has been identified as that of PETER LEITH, 22, of Noordgate. AGNES LEITH (mother of the deceased) was able to confirm his identity on Monday. Mr. Leith's body was discovered face downward in the marsh below the east-most floodgate by Ignis X. Gullstrand, Porbeagle's lamplighter, on the morning of the 28th. Investigations have concluded Leith was a victim of alcohol. A coroner's jury found that his death was a case of accidental drowning.

———————

Granna shifts to the kitchen. She puts some bread in the toaster and begins to sing. She used to sing well, she often tells Candle. A leadlight prism hangs in the window casting rainbow flame-shapes across the sand-coloured surfaces.

'I'm going out with him tonight,' Candle says to Granna, too quietly for her to hear. 'To light the lamps.'

Granna, with the coloured lights shifting all around her, sings with all her heart.

Aquarium

Candle leaves Granna's flat without saying goodbye. On the road to the aquarium he takes out his remaining talismans, one at a time. The ring. The fossil. A shrunken green tomato. Granna's string of fake pearls. But they're all powerless—Peter Leith is beyond their help. Even the great white shark tooth grows dull in his hand. He takes out the Waywarden's moon powder. He pries open the zip-lock and jiggles the bag to loosen the stuff inside.

It'll make you feel good.

Candle stops on the road. He tips some powder into the palm of his hand. He tips a little more. Satisfied with the dosage he brings it to his mouth and licks it from his palm. He licks again to clean up the residue. Candle puts the bag away and keeps on walking. The sun grows hot on his shoulders.

———————

CANDLE ENTERS THE AQUARIUM, alone in the dark. His head is a flame, and generates its own light. He is illuminated,—

When he enters he approaches a viewing window. It takes up a whole wall. He can't see through the swirling grey smoke inside, but he knows there are sea creatures in the smoke; it's an aquarium after all. The haze breaks apart as a huge form glides by. Candle follows its tail fins through the glass and into the aquarium.

Inside, the haze breaks apart. At the centre of the chamber stands a gargantuan column, of coral and flowers made from skin and blood. The column has heaving breasts, tremendous thighs, and an arm with a hand on the end—holding onto a champagne flute.

'Hail,' says the column in Emerald's voice. 'We give thanks.'

'The night, the flood,' call voices from all around, 'is black, is foul.'

Candle walks the aquarium floor. Around him giant black angelfish, with bulbous blind eyes, circle the column. Glowing lanterns dangle from fleshly stalks sprouting at their heads. One lantern implodes—*Fffowh*—and a cloud of glassy shards drifts to the floor.

Candle moves from the chamber into an underwater passageway. His head flame reveals recesses in the passage walls, like shrines. Each recess contains a brain coral. He leans close to one.

'Let's have it then, shall we?' it says.

Below the coral, a plaque on the walls reads, KEMP TIBALD. The next one, SIGI AHN.

'A flame in the shape of a heart,' it says. 'In honour of your granddad.'

'Ignis, Ignis, Ignis, Ignis,' sighs the next brain. The plaque reads GIL.

As Candle makes his way down the passageway, an octopus, like a head of hair, emerges from within a dressing gown and swims away. Candle's light trembles. A sea snake hesitantly samples the inside of a porcelain pill cup with its tongue. At the end of the passageway someone raises his or her hand in greeting.

'Walk backwards towards her,' says Waverly De Vol. Her little ones, Sweetheart and Hal, are hiding behind her dress, which billows in the current. When Candle reaches her, she gives him a fish the size of a hand mirror, or a hand mirror in the shape of a fish. 'Only look at the reflection,' advises Waverly.

There is a bend, an entrance, a portal. A conveyor belt pulls Candle through the threshold into a tunnel. Ahead is the platform. Waverly's fish orbits his bright head, sending beams of light into the kelp forest behind the glass.

'Candle,' calls a voice like his mother's, when he steps onto the platform.

He walks backwards towards her.

'These are some of our fearful things.'

On the polished silver surface of Waverly's fish, Candle sees his mother. Her shipwreck-coloured hair fans out and intertwines with the kelp. The blacks of her eyes are big. She sits naked on a sunken crate.

Candle turns to face her. An octopus like a head of hair startles, and says, 'Candle—behind you.'

In the aquarium glass between himself and his mother, Candle sees the reflection of a dog with the face of a man.

'Come to me,' it barks.

'Candle, what are you doing down there?'

The Aquarama dolphin pool, at the back of the aquarium complex, hasn't been used for years. The outdoor grandstand was dismantled when the last resident dolphin died of old age and the pool was drained. Even so, Candle is in up to his knees. The substrate collected in the pool bottom is part leaf litter, part stagnant water. Rib notices a heat-seeking leech inching up the material of Candle's pants. He calls again. 'Candle?'

Candle turns in the sludge.

'Your van's locked,' he says. 'I followed an aquarium cat.' And then, 'I was going to wait for you here.'

Rib takes off his sailor cap, in case it falls in the muck. He climbs down the ladder and helps Candle out. On dry land he picks the leech from the hem of Candle's pants and chucks it to the audience of aquarium cats. The tabby pounces.

Rib drives his van past the pastures and dairy farms that make up the space between Anchorite and Porbeagle. They're halfway home.

'Candle, are you going to tell me what you took?'

'Yeah, Rib,' he says. 'I'm okay.'

'That's not what I asked.' Rib sighs. 'Do you want to stay over tonight? We could talk about what's bothering you. Or we could just watch TV.' Rib moves a hand from the steering wheel as if to reach for Candle. Candle crosses his arms.

'I can't,' he says. 'I'm lamplighting.'

The Dark Road

THE STOPBANK SNAKES OUT IN FRONT OF IGNIS.

It stops the swamp from reclaiming the settled land, and Porbeagle was all swamp once. That was a long time ago. The land on the right side of the bank has grown used to being above water.

The Lamplighter looks sideways at where he thinks Candle should be, a few paces behind him. He's not there. Must still be back at the river bridge.

'C'mon, Candle,' says Ignis, trying to throw his voice all the way back to the bridge. It's a quiet enough night for that, but the words catch in his dentures, on his dry tongue. Ahead of him, all along the stopbank, for as far as it reaches, Ignis can see his lamps. It's not good. Some of them have gone out. There are dark gaps in his light.

Ignis pulls at the cork in his lemonade bottle. He drinks.

'Candle!' Better, louder that time. He calls again, 'C'mon, Candle!'

As if in answer, comes the shattering of glass. It's a terrible sound. The sound of a lantern falling apart. He turns around in time to see the light on the underbelly of the bridge go dark. It takes him a moment to understand, and then his heart sinks in his chest. Candle is breaking the lamps. Ignis lurches forward, charging towards the bridge. Up ahead, Candle reaches another lamppost, and stops. Ignis sees him reach for his pocket—and another lamp goes out. He's throwing rocks. He's putting out the lamplight.

'Candle,' Ignis roars. 'Candle, stop!'

Candle has put out another two lamps before Ignis can reach him. Ignis avalanches. He descends on his grandson, seizing him by the shoulders with huge hands.

'What're you doing that for?' hisses Ignis. 'Why?' His voice cracks. His lungs harden, becoming two stones in his chest.

The boy's face is clenched. His lips are barely parted, barely showing his teeth. He's trying to not let his fear show.

'Can you feel him moving?' says Candle.

Ignis stares. Candle struggles in his grip.

'I'm letting him in—Peter Leith.'

Ignis throws Candle from him, lifting him from the bank and into the air. There's a dull metal sound when his body strikes the lamppost—Candle rolls down the bank, out of sight. Ignis steadies himself, and eyes his grandson. Waist deep in the bog, Candle is moving into the dark of the willow forest. He's clutching his shoulder.

'Get back here,' Ignis shouts. 'You'll bloody drown! Get back here, you little shit!'

Candle has moved out of the lamplight. Ignis skids down the bank, losing his footing towards the bottom. His feet hit the bog and his boots fill up with water. He wades out. Gripping his pole by the very end, he holds it into the dark, struggling to keep it aloft. The small light at the end has no power without a lamp to activate. He stumbles in the mud. The end of the pole hits the water surface and goes out.

'Candle,' Ignis calls limply into the willows. Nothing.

133

The Lamplighter wades back to the bank. As he goes, he lifts each foot right out of the water, as if to dry it for a moment, before plunging it back into the bog. He reaches dry land and clambers up the bank to the top. He waits under the pool of lamplight, catching his breath, looking towards the village. Eventually he sees a shadow emerge from the darkness at the floodgate. The shadow moves into each circle of light left under the remaining lamps. Eventually he's out of sight. Ignis shoulders his extinguished pole, and starts back home.

Stopbank

Engines with clamp claws and track tyres drive through the pastures to reach the stopbank, sending the livestock into spooked huddles at the far corners of their fields.

The men and their machines begin by prying lampposts from the earth, piling them up by the floodgate, like blown-out birthday candles. Later, a dump truck arrives, and they're loaded onto the back and taken away.

Along one side of the stopbank the waywardens dig a trench. Certain points along the way are pegged. A smallish engine is brought in, brandishing a spire-sized auger at the end of a robotic arm. It teeters from one end of the stopbank to the other, pausing to sink its weapon deep into the earth at every peg marker.

At the end of the week, the truck that took the old lampposts away returns with a stack of hollow aluminium columns. A power cable will soon run through each column; at its top, a bracket will be attached to hold an electric light. The columns go up quickly, in the holes left by the auger. Heavy-duty black cables are laid along the bottom of the trench, running between each column. The trench is then filled with a layer of fresh gravel, a warning stripe of red tape, and then more backfill, dirt familiar to the wetland.

Finally the waywardens tidy up their machines, sipping

on bottles of beer as they work—the new lights aren't functional yet, but the holidays start tomorrow, and they'll pick things up from where they left off in the new year. One of the waywardens—the tall man, with the moon powder—is the last to shepherd his machine across the pasture. In his hurry, eager to return home to a hot shower, he forgets to close the gates between each field. He has a go at the last gate, looping the length of cord through the wire links of the gate and around the last post of the adjoining fence. He ties a knot, which almost immediately loosens. He leaves it like that, and stalks off to join the other waywardens. They leave Porbeagle.

Plantation

It's Christmas Eve morning.

Sylla is picking up pinecones from the forest floor, placing some in her bucket, discarding others. At home she'll paint the ones she keeps. She'll tie them with ribbons and hang them to dry above the fireplace, in windows, and in the branches of the Christmas tree. She'll pack the bucket with river rocks to keep the tree steady.

Candle and Rib are sitting on the boot of the car, watching Sylla slink through the shade at the plantation edge. Gil has gone deeper into the forest to look for a Christmas tree-sized sapling.

Before Candle was made apprentice to his grandfather, his dad would take him here to go hunting. Gil would wake the sun up, and Candle would eat breakfast for a change—porridge, brown sugar, bitter milky tea—and the taste of it would be in his mouth all morning. They'd never get anything. The forest would be empty. The stag was a footprint at the edge of a stream, its existence always inconclusive. Candle suspected these father–son trips were never meant to end with a kill. He guessed now that his father knew him, even then, better than Candle had ever given him credit for.

'I think my dad should get a dog,' says Candle to Rib. The sun is up and warming the body of the car. Rib stretches.

'Yeah,' he says. 'He might need a friend if you leave Porbeagle. He should get a dog.'

Candle is thinking about shifting, maybe to Hellgrammite, or even further away. The Lamplighter's retirement party is tonight. The thought of his grandfather with more time on his hands, more time to spend drinking, is enough of an incentive to leave.

'Would you come with me?'

'I left Porbeagle once,' says Rib, lying back on the windscreen with his eyes closed. 'I came back.'

Candle shrugs. He's already mentioned the idea to Sylla, and she said no. Candle wasn't asking for her permission.

'You need to talk to your mum,' murmurs Rib. 'About Peter.'

'I know.'

Candle has told only Rib about what Granna had shown him. Since he smashed the lanterns he has quit the dark road, which is what Sylla asked him to do anyway. She hasn't spoken to her father since the fairgrounds. The Lamplighter has been avoiding all contact, staying hidden up in his house on stilts.

Gil comes back with a felled sapling on his shoulder. Rib helps him tie it to the roof, with enthusiasm, eager to please. Candle watches his dad warm to Rib's charm.

'Where's your mum, Candle?' says Gil, working on the last knot. 'She's wandered off.'

Candle sees her through the trees. She's resting against a tree trunk. Two fantails wheel around her in erratic orbits. Sylla watches her son approach.

'Mum—'

'What is it?' she says.

'I'll tell you when we get home.' Candle offers her his hand, and she takes it. They walk back to the car.

Porbeagle Row

'No,' Sylla says. She's leaning against the glass sliding door that opens to the front deck. There's fury on her face; she's fused like a sphinx. 'Wet Pete isn't real.'

'Peter Leith was.' Candle is on the beanbag, facing her. 'Granna showed me the newspaper clipping. Granddad found the body.'

'She shouldn't have told you that. Why did she?'

'It's terrible, Mum. But it shouldn't have been kept a secret.'

'Dad might've not killed him. He can't have meant it to happen like that.'

'I don't think he meant for Peter to die, but Pan and him went to the bridge for a reason. Something did happen.'

Sylla's hand becomes a fist. It flies backwards and smashes into the pane of glass that's supporting her. The picture-of-outside pixellates—grape hyacinths, snowball-shaped flowers, a rope swing tied to a kanuka, the swampbrink and the wetland beyond—and obliterates, falling all around her.

'Sylla!' bellows Gil from the kitchen, his voice full of fear and love. Candle is stunned. He shrinks to the centre of the beanbag, although most of the glass has fallen outside.

Sylla brings her arm to her lap. The back of her hand is split open. An ugly cut begins to turn scarlet. She keens in grief; she closes her eyes and tilts back her chin and a sound comes out like a separate thing, like a bad spirit.

'Where's the first aid kit, Candle?' Gil is crouching by Sylla. He helps her up. 'Find it!'

It's not on top of the fridge. Candle looks under the sink, then in the laundry cupboard—it's on the top shelf. He takes it to the bathroom. Gil has Sylla sitting on the edge of the bathtub rinsing her hand under the tap. Her blood turns orange as it circles the drain. Candle pries the lid from the kit and gives it to his dad, who sets it in the basin. Sylla sobs quietly while Gil cleans and dresses her wound. Candle watches from the door.

Sylla's Bedroom

CANDLE IS THE ONLY ONE HOME.

Sylla has left the house; Gil followed after her. The three of them were supposed to go to the village hall together, to attend the Lamplighter's retirement. It isn't likely Sylla will make it. Granna won't be there either; neither will Wynell, nor Undine. The light is leaving the sky. Eventide is approaching.

In his bedroom Candle pulls his childhood dollhouse from a corner. He opens the front piece. The floor space is flurried with an entire wardrobe of doll outfits, doll furniture, doll cutlery and crockery, glossy meals fused to dishes, and other miscellaneous home dressings. The tenants, furry cat and dog figurines, float in the debris. There's an attic space, which is clear and unoccupied, except for a real-life pickle jar. It's sinister sitting there by itself, as if its contents might be behind the disarray downstairs. Candle picks it up and holds it up to the light. Inside a jellyfish has dissolved and turned the seawater bright blue. Candle handles the pickle jar gingerly and checks that the screw cap is on tight. He places it on his chest of drawers and undresses.

He takes a bath. Afterwards, instead of towelling himself dry and putting on his clothes, he goes to his mum and dad's room, to Sylla's dresser. At the mirror he dips into the pottles, and presses fingerprints of day cream and night cream onto his warm damp skin. He moves the tweezers as if to pluck any stray hair. He tests the crocheted hand pump of the empty perfume bottle and receives its last breath on his collarbone. Inside a red plastic clamshell he discovers a pallet of moist shimmering powders and a minuscule swab, which he uses to dab the powder to his skin and around his eyes. He tries the waxy pencils, and the Sylla-coloured stuff in a tube. He draws circles on his skin. He mottles himself, as if with sunlight, or pond decay, or the markings of sea creatures with full and colourful venom at their ready. He draws a red circle on the circle of his lips. Once he is done, once he is something like satisfied, he climbs into his underwear, and into the rust-coloured silk. He takes the pickle jar from the chest of drawers and leaves the house to meet Rib at the beach.

Porbeagle

It's approaching eventide, but the air is still warm, there is still light in the sky. The Lamplighter stands alone on the beach. Above him sea birds are coming in from a day or more away on the open ocean, to roost in the salt-warped macrocarpa pines that stand between the coast and the village. First the birds come in pairs, then in threes or fours. They're pied shags, black-backed gulls, an intrepid heron. But it's not long before the main body of the seafarers return and then the sky is filled. The gulls cry like creaking doors as they descend on the topmost boughs of the pines. And following after, as if reined in by the birds, comes a front of thick sea mist. The Lamplighter staggers back up the dunes and disappears under cover of the pine forest.

––––––––

EMERALD TAPUWAI ARRIVES AT PORBEAGLE HALL at quarter to six. Barb Grig has closed the shop early and is waiting for Emerald inside. She has hooked back the double doors at the entrance and is turning on the interior lights.

'Hail, Emerald,' calls Barb.

Emerald is silent. She paces the length of the empty hall.

'Well,' says Barb, 'we might be in for a whiteout tonight, mightn't we?'

Emerald isn't listening.

'Fog's a brewing, that's for sure,' says Barb.

Sigi Ahn shows up to unfold and lay out the trestle tables. By eventide the Zip boiler is bubbling, and the villagers are beginning to fill up the hall. The polished particleboard floor tiles squeak under more and more pairs of sand shoes. Singed dust drifts down from the hanging lights. Already somebody has spilled a soft drink near the service kitchenette. The puddle has been wiped up, but a sticky residue remains on the floor.

The Lamplighter doesn't arrive, but a photographer from the *Anchorite Chronicle* does. His name badge reads 'U. Dilley'. He clutches at his camera, while Barb and Seabright move platters of saveloys and olives and cockles and pineapple—all skewered together on toothpicks— around the crêpe paper-swaddled trestles. Kemp Tibald raps his cane on the floor and says, 'Let's have it then, shall we?' The photographer takes out a spiral-bound notepad. Ted Weatherly says to him, 'It's hard to find men like Ignis these days,' and his wife Valerie mutters, 'It's a bloody good thing too.' U. Dilley notes this down.

'Until the man of the hour arrives, might I speak to a family member?' enquires the photographer, gravitating towards the still point of the room, Emerald Tapuwai.

'None of them have shown up, I'm afraid,' she replies, evenly.

Barb Grig guides U. Dilley aside to have quiet words. She can't contain some of them though. 'The night, the flood, is black, is foul,' she cries. And then, 'Avaunt!' U. Dilley leaves then. He decides not to take a photograph.

It's a little after seven when Emerald mounts the podium. The Lamplighter hasn't come to see out his retirement. For

145

the sake of morale, and for the sake of an ending, Emerald has decided to conduct a search.

'Hail, Porbeagle,' she calls, addressing the congregation.

'Hail yourself, woman,' calls back Kemp Tibald.

Emerald's hair is in a warrior's braid. She's wearing a long sleeveless kaftan, displaying her powerful arms. She gives Kemp a look as if she would run him through with a javelin if she could get her hands on one.

'We,' she says, 'are gathered here to give thanks to the Lamplighter. He isn't here.' Emerald pauses. She runs the tip of her tongue over her front teeth. The hall is silent for a moment before she continues. 'In order to conclude the Lamplighter's service to the community we must deliver him to his reception.'

Emerald Tapuwai, villagehead and remnant of an old Porbeagle family, stands under a flickering electric light on the porch of the general store. Her bare arms are goose-pimpled. She looks into the dark sea smoke as it moves by in undulating and elephantine drifts.

Barb Grig has led a band of women in the direction of the house on stilts. There they find a flock of escaped sheep dining on apples and crab apples, and an empty house. The sliding door is open a crack, but on investigation nobody is home. Before they leave, Barb sees that something has been thrown against the side of the house, leaving a slimy mark. The bright blue fluid has oozed down the wall and is dripping onto the remains of a pickle jar below.

Ted Weatherly drives his wife Valerie, slowly and carefully through the fog, to the Spruce & Spritz on the chance that the Lamplighter has stopped by for a refreshment or two. He hasn't, but a table is free by the electric fireplace, so they sit down for a roast meal.

At the lagoon, under the water's surface, a stingray the size of a tractor tyre swoops across the sandy bottom, from burrow to burrow. At each hole in the mud it vacuums out the occupying crab, turning it around in its maw and scattering the leftovers. On shore, Sigi Ahn checks each boatshed. Emerald's glass-bottomed dinghy is missing.

Sigi sees the light of a torch and finds Keeley Samuelson with his Labrador, Jess. They cross the lagoon mudflat together and trace the bank of the river to its mouth. The beam of bluish light from Keeley's torch cuts through the fog ahead of them like a laser. Where the fog is at its thickest the beam becomes more distinct, more material than anything else. At the mouth Keeley hears the creaking of oars.

'That you out there rowing, Gil?' utters Keeley.

'Yep, it is,' returns a voice from the fog. 'Just out with Sylla for a turn on the lagoon.'

'Howdy, Sylla,' says Keeley. 'Isn't this fog something?'

'Certainly is, Keeley,' says Sylla. 'You'll watch your step walking out here at night, won't you?'

'That's good advice,' says Keeley. 'Sigi and I'll be heading back to the village now.'

'Sigi too! I can't see a thing,' says Gil.

The four exchange their goodnights and head their separate ways back home. In the dinghy Sylla unravels the bandage wrapped around her hand. At first the cloth is white, but soon a red spot appears, which increases in size layer after layer.

'Love, what are you doing?' Gil keeps rowing.

Sylla pulls away the bandage and drops it overboard, like an offering.

'Avaunt,' she whispers. 'Avaunt, Wet Pete.'

Seabright Durivage hands Emerald a shawl, and then a mug of hot soup. She turns to leave, back across the road to her bungalow and her husband.

'Seabright,' calls Emerald, unmoving at the shop front. 'How's Romuald's face?'

'He's got a whopper bruise,' ventures the former shopkeeper, calling over her shoulder. 'But he'll be okay. He doesn't want any trouble.'

Emerald nods. Seabright disappears into the mist and Emerald gathers the shawl around her shoulders, takes a sip of the thin silvery soup. She listens. The seabirds are still making noises as they settle in for the night; otherwise Porbeagle is quiet. The villagers are conducting the search for the Lamplighter in silence. Emerald had expected to hear his name perforating the mist, along with hails and avaunts. But no, just the birds.

There are one hundred and eight properties in Porbeagle; thirty-five cottages, seventy-one houses, one general store, one village hall. Emerald doubts the Lamplighter is to be found in any of them. Normally at this time of night he'd be starting down the swampbrink, lighting his lamps. But not tonight. The nights since his lampposts were pulled from the stopbank have been the first nights in decades that the swampbrink has been left dark.

Kemp Tibald joins Emerald on the porch. He'd stayed in the hall while the search parties formed, and only now has he come out into the night. Kemp was once friends with Emerald's father. He was once considered for the role of lamplighter. Nowadays he looks something like Ignis. Shabby. An old toothless lion.

'Well then,' says Kemp, punctuating the words with a rap of his cane on the concrete steps. There are splatters all down his front, red wine spills, or beetroot juice.

Delilah. Emerald imagines the word, or another—*deceiver* or *harpy* or *bitch*—coagulating on his tongue. Ready to be spat out.

'I've cut us loose,' she says. 'I had to.'

Kemp grunts. He spits out a question mark instead. It hits the concrete with a splat.

'We were tethered to a broken horse, Kemp. Tethered to a broken tradition. There was nothing else for it.'

The old man produces a bottle from the interior pocket of his coat and lifts it to his mouth. The bottle balances on his lips, bubbles rising as the wine gurgles into his mouth. Kemp's not like a lion now, more like a suckling calf. He could be a lamppost and the bottle of wine a lantern glass gone dark.

Just then there is a squeal of tyres. On the corner a car has appeared out of the mist. In the headlights a Friesian heifer has stepped onto the road. The occupant of the car toots and the heifer moves, only to be replaced by another. A third cow and then a fourth appear. Their barrel-shaped bodies form an ambling blockade against the car, which inches forwards and toots a second time. The cattle startle. The first heifer staggers forward, tossing its forequarters in the air, breaking into a run. One cow moans achingly, another makes a sound like a roar. Their hooves clatter on the road surface. The herd gallops past the shop front, past

Emerald and Kemp, and under cover of the mist they move in the direction of the wetland.

Waverly De Vol walks the dark road alone. In the gloom the wetland swells in size; its presence becomes dizzying. It feels like she's walking along a cliff's edge. It's not pitch black, however. A big moon shows through gaps in the sea smoke that's spreading over the marshes. On the way here she stopped by her garden to pick a bunch of grape hyacinths. She drops a flower every so often along the stopbank. At the floodgate she leaves several. She doesn't know where it was exactly that her twins entered the wetland sixteen years ago. They had drowned nonetheless.

Waverly hears cows on the move in the distance. She keeps walking. At the river bridge one lamp is alight, the last of the old lampposts left standing. It must have been missed by the waywardens, or not bothered with. The flame is shaking and feeble, in spasm against the concrete underbelly of the bridge; the lantern is missing glass. The Lamplighter is standing underneath. He has his back to Waverly, leaning on his post, letting his pole droop. Overhead a stock truck rushes past. The rest of the grape hyacinths fall from Waverly's hand. She turns back down the dark road and walks home.

The Beach

Candle crosses the pine forest to get to the beach.

He's moving in darkness, but he knows the sandy trail well. Under brief spells of moonlight, parts of the woods are revealed and the tree trunks become fragrant as they gradually drench, engulfed in the sea smoke.

Candle is about to cross from the woods into the dunes, but he stops. Behind him, back down the path, something is coming closer. He can feel it moving towards him, through vibrations in the fog, or through the pads of his feet. He stumbles off the path, crouches,—

He hears them breathing first, before he sees them. The Porbeagle mares move from the forest out into the open, murmuring as they tread, reassuring one another. The moonlight strengthens through a dilute mass of cloud and one mare, the matriarch, throws back her mane and leads her flock onto the beach at a run. The foal—the most beautiful, the most perfect—comes last, splashing through the mist like a thing part fish and part flame.

———————

CANDLE REBOUNDS FROM THE SEABED. Glittery specks swarm around him like dust in a bright room. As he approaches the surface, blobs of air squeeze through his lips and rise ahead of him. He lifts his head to the surface and gasps for air. In the dark, even with the mist clearing and the moon out, it's not easy to place the world. Candle waits for a swell to move him, and then follows it back to shore.

Candle steps through inches of water, into the arms of Rib.

'You swam by yourself,' Rib says. 'Where are your clothes?'

They walk up the beach and find where Candle left his things. He wriggles his feet into his underwear and slips on his rust-coloured silk.

'Will you wait for me at your house?'

'Where will you be?'

'I need to graduate from my apprenticeship,' says Candle. 'I need to become extinct.'

Porbeagle Hall

The Lamplighter hasn't come to see out his retirement.

The search parties have reassembled inside the hall. The escaped animals—the sheep, cows, and horses—will need to be rounded up and restored to the pasture, but nobody has the energy for that tonight. It can wait until the morning.

Emerald is weary. She has Sigi move the tables and chairs to the edges of the hall while she shifts a crate to the centre space. A bar heater is plugged in and begins to glow orange. Emerald lets her hair out and undresses. She gathers her body into a pose that will be remembered for generations: one foot on the floor, one on the crate; muscles shift like pockets of magma underneath the skin of her arms as she flexes and clasps her hands behind her back; her hair, in a burgundy current, falls over her left shoulder, covering one entire breast. Initially the villagers might have been unenthusiastic, but Emerald has a spectacular form, and it's something to do. They take up their easels and begin to draw.

CANDLE ENTERS THE HALL with seawater still on his body. He leaves damp footprints.

Emerald lets out a breath when she sees him come in. She

relaxes her body, relinquishing her place, and Candle drops his silk. His body is a long piece of willow, sea polished, and bumpy in the places where his bones show through. He's still speckled with the residue of Sylla's makeup. His shipwreck-coloured hair seems longer and clings to the nape of his neck. Candle closes his eyes, tilts his chin to the ceiling.

One by one the villagers turn over their sheets and make record of the new, brief, and last lamplighter of Porbeagle.

Porbeagle Row

IT IS NEW YEAR'S MORNING. The Christmas tree rusts in the living room.

Sylla's empty breakfast tray sits in the kitchen. A porcelain cup holds an assortment of different coloured pills and jelly tablets.

She has been quiet for days, tending her hens and her garden. She has lifted some boxes from storage, sifted through the contents, and put them away again. This morning she sits Candle down. She brings him a photograph, of a young child in a little dress, poking at a thing in the mud—a moon jelly? A man kneeling with her in a singlet and shorts scrutinises the thing, smiling down at her. It's a sideways view of him—he looks like Peter Leith, vibrantly alive alongside the girl that is Candle's mother. Such a bright pretty thing she had been. Her hair had never been cut. Her sharp white teeth. Her green eyes full of sunlight.

'Peter wasn't just a stranger under the bridge,' says Sylla. 'I remember him.'

Candle stands up, but Sylla reaches for his hand and stops him. He leans into her shoulder. He imagines men, not unlike himself, meeting under the river bridge at night, to lay fishing lines in dark currents, and to light fires, and to be alone together in the willow forest. He pictures his grandfather—a beautiful young man, and still a candle then—lingering at the periphery, holding a pole with a bright light at the end, and beginning to tell himself a story, about a lone bushman and a mountaintop lake.

Sylla cradles her son's head in her hands.

River Bridge

CANDLE walks along the stopbank at night with Rib. They're both wearing head torches. Their breath comes up into their lights, huge hot wisps, like from extinguished wicks.

'Look at you and me,' says Rib. 'A pair of candles.'

They go to the river bridge. The doggod calls to them—a soft, indistinct sound—but they don't listen, and it retreats back into the broom scrub. In the fire pit under the bridge they make their sacrifices: a water-damaged dedication clipped out of a newspaper; clippings from other, older newspapers, headed 'body found' and 'body named'; and a prayer card with Michael pushing Lucifer into the mud. A photograph. Of a little girl, of a young man. These items are placed in the ashes. Candle pours lamp oil and—*hwofff*—lights a fire.

I wish I could describe the burning of each item to you now. I wish I had the eyes and the words for that. Well, what is burning, but a quick, hot decay?

Will that do?

Acknowledgements

My heartfelt thanks to the students and faculty at the International Institute of Modern Letters. Thanks in particular to Kate Duignan, under whose guidance I seeded the ideas for this book in 2011, and Damien Wilkins, for your humour and warm heartedness, and for pouring the fertiliser over the top. My deep gratitude to Denis and Verna Adam for their support in finishing this book.

To my 2012 class—Cushla Managh, Helen Innes, Georgia Vaughan, Megan Doyle Corcoran, Samantha Byres, Sarah Jane Parton, Sue Francis, Wendy Nolan and Lydia Wisheart—my heartfelt thanks for your brains and generosity, and for the oat-free banquets. It has been a pleasure and privilege to write with you all.

Many, many thanks to all the wonderful people at VUP. Special thanks to Fergus Barrowman, for your confidence and for the care you've taken with *Lamplighter*, and Ashleigh Young for making the editing process so memorable and fun.

Thank you to all those involved with Zealandia, the Karori Wildlife Sanctuary, where I wrote much of *Lamplighter*, and continue to look to for inspiration and retreat.

To my family and friends, it has been with your love and support that I've written this book.

I would like to acknowledge the LGBTQ people, from Aotearoa and abroad, who navigated less friendly seas than I, and who have persevered and fought for the freedoms I enjoy today.